Also by Fred Sokol

Fiction
Destiny
Mendel and Morris
Silverbirch Summer

Plays
The Forever Boys
The Lewis Sisters

Non Fiction
Muses in Arcadia: Cultural Life in the Berkshires
(co-author)

Praise for Fred Sokol's Work

Five Star Reviews

Silverbirch Summer

The book follows a few months in the life of April between high school and college in 1965. She lies about her age to get a job teaching basketball (Celtic's great Bob Cousy is her inspiration) at Silverbirch camp and meets an eclectic group of people. Her childhood best friend suddenly turned boyfriend is also added into the mix. Told from April's pov and will appeal to adults and young adults who enjoy historical fiction. ~Amazon Reader

Mendel and Morris

Not only are the characters a hoot; so are many of the predicaments they get themselves into. But this book also takes a serious look at the opportunities and limitations of old age, which may slow us down even as it opens new doors and renews our appetite for living. Sokol has a real talent for writing realistic yet distinctive dialogue. By the end I had grown to love the characters and wanted the story to continue; I hope a sequel is in the works. Readers of all ages will enjoy Mendel and Morris. ~Massachusetts Reader

Destiny

Philip Roth meets William Blake (and, every so often, Gabriel Garcia Marquez) in this hilarious, heartwarming sequel to Fred Sokol's debut novel Mendel and Morris. The "M&M Boys," retired seventy-something Jewish widowers and bosom buddies, find unexpected adventure and enlightenment on a road trip across the Bay State from their Springfield home to Cape Ann on the North Shore. With their contemporary shuffleboard-champion (also Jewish) housemates, the Lewis sisters (Gilda and Zena), and several younger companions, they kvetch their way toward a multiple new "Destiny." Readers of a certain age will kvell to a mid-twentieth-century soundtrack ranging from the Beatles to "Fiddler on the Roof." Fans of its predecessor will find the same snappy dialogue and good humor, along with deeper character exploration (who knew a leading player kept a diary?) and a bold new strain of mysticism, in this wise and winning successor. A highly recommended read for all ages.

ISBN: 979-8-9859106-3-6

Destiny is a work of fiction. Names, characters, places and incidents are the product of the author's imagination or are used fictitiously and are not to be construed as real. Any resemblance to actual events, locations, organizations or persons, living or dead, is entirely coincidental.

Anatevka Press

88 Westmoreland Avenue

Longmeadow, MA 01106

For Ron Berenson

"I write to find out about myself"

Stephen King

Revisiting—June 2011

HARRY AND CAROLYN HAD now been together for nearly forty years as marrieds. He thought it likely and logical that their union had endured, and she could only attribute the relationship's survival to fate.

They did agree that their daughters provided both impetus and glue when the personal fabric occasionally frayed. Marissa and Diana were paramount in their minds: They adored the kids whom they wished would provide grandchildren. Marissa lived nearby in Brooklyn, while Diana was in Moab, Utah. Harry and Carolyn had long ago journeyed to that southwestern town and wound up getting married there. Reflecting on their union, Carolyn concluded that near breaks occurred all too often while Harry, even now, minimized each fracture.

It was time to re-experience the nuclear unit with their girls. It had been four decades since Harry and Carolyn had temporarily fled their Houston Street apartment in Manhattan for a week to hike among the red rocks of the Southwest. Now, flying through the skies to Moab, Utah, the two thought back to that time—

Part I

Chapter 1

New York

Summer 1970

HEAT BLASTED HARRY FROM above and below as he emerged from the subway and walked toward East Houston Street. But he could not find number twenty-four, and he was in a panic. Wearing a striped shirt and shorts, his hair held in place by a bandana, Harry's pores could not hold that much water. He knew he smelled. On this, the first morning of his stint as a census taker amid a heat wave, he would stink up the place. What place? Where was the building? They told him it was a tenement. Big help. All of these apartment structures, some without visible numbers, left him guessing as to the location. Frustrated and sweating profusely, Harry sat down on the sidewalk.

Having grown up in the suburbs (a "bridge and tunnel" boy), Harry was in awe of Manhattan. While he pretended to understand street grids, he was oftentimes confused. He looked up at the concrete and brick structures and sighed. A girl with frizzy red hair who was jogging with her dog called out,

"Hey, what's up? You okay?" As she paused, the dog licked Harry's face.

"Just can't find number twenty-four," said Harry.

"It's back a block. Indented—you know, like in English class. I mean, set back. See?" She pointed as Harry stood, peered, and noticed that the projection of buildings was standing forward as if a complete row was permanently altered. "That's it. That's the one you want. See you," the girl said and moved on. He turned, but it seemed like everyone was heading toward him. It added up to Harry versus a stampede of New Yorkers eager to get through the first weekend of July and into their customary and preferred style of life.

It wasn't supposed to be a solo gig. Sandy had the notion that he and Harry could grab census jobs, earn some good money, and spend some time together once again. As very best friends in college, each had gone off on their own after graduation. The plan was that they would now resume as what they considered themselves to be: brothers. Harry had signed on, and then Sandy died. Kaput. Harry did not easily survive the knockout blow. He was thinking of Sandy as he battled through throngs of early morning workers. The girl with the captivating swatch of bright red hair had vanished in the opposite direction. Harry muttered to himself. If he and Carolyn had not decided to take the summer off, maybe he wouldn't be pushing through the crowd searching for a building that may not even exist. He told Carolyn he was fine with a short separation, but he desperately missed her.

Harry used a rolled-up issue of *The Saturday Review* to forge his way. It had two articles he kept reading over and over—the one Irving Howe wrote, which pissed him off so, about how The New Left was not quite what it thought; and the measured piece about Bob Dylan. He had memorized the title: "Poetry of Salvation."

Right now, though, he was less concerned with the magazine's content than he was with its ability to help him get to a building with an affixed two and a dangling four by the front door. Maybe this was the place: It was significantly set back, which fit the girl's description. Harry turned abruptly and walked to the front door, where he was greeted with a message asking that he hold down a button, choose the correct apartment number, and state his purpose.

Harry went for the first apartment and said, "My name is Harry Falkman, and I'm taking census. Can I please come in?"

No response. He pressed, successively, numbers two and three and did not get replies. Harry knew he had to get into the building. He saw an accessible window that must lead to a resident's apartment. Standing on tiptoe, Harry tapped and then banged on it. He thought he saw a man's shadowed face in the background, and then the area around the front door buzzed. Harry scrambled to grab and turn the front door handle. The heavy door snapped open, and he fell forward.

It was suddenly comparatively cool. Harry gathered himself, tried to adjust his hair and then approached Apartment One. He rapped on the door twice. It sounded like someone was coming but then thought better of it. As sweat dried on him, Harry wondered whether to simply bag this whole insane project. He wiped his forehead and remembered the crumpled New York Mets cap he had stuffed into his back pocket. Harry lifted the bandana, replaced it with the hat, and hoped this would make him a bit more presentable. The door opened just a crack and a voice asked, "What do you want?"

His throat stuck, but Harry managed to answer, "I'm taking census." He looked at his script and tried to recite it verbatim. "This is an important time, and we request that you answer the following questions to the best of your ability." He hesitated and added, "Okay?"

The voice answered, "No one else here," just as the cry of a child pierced the air. Harry was not certain which apartment it had come from. He knew he would have to cajole the person on the other side of the door to cooperate. "Listen, I'm just a kid trying to do a job," Harry said. "Could you please come out?" Hearing a familiar lock and chain noise, Harry continued, "I just don't want to mess this up."

As the locking mechanism further released and yielded, there stood a man whose unlined face held a grizzled, dark beard with an occasional speck of gray. His smile was welcoming. "Sure, come in," he said. "I just wanted to make certain nobody was hassling me. I can easily see that's not you."

Harry, pleased to be invited inside, tripped over the door sill, dropping his clipboard on the floor as papers flew in all directions. He looked the man in the eye, and both began laughing. The man's hands fluttered as he mimicked the scattering pages and said, warmly and cordially, "How can I be helpful?"

"I need figures for the 1970 census. I mean, there's this expectation that you get to so many places in a day. I couldn't find you to save myself."

Coughing, the man said, "I live in a palace, as you can well see. For you, getting these details right is where it's at. I can appreciate that since I was good at math and even stepped in to teach it not that many years ago."

The easy tone of the conversation allowed Harry to relax and actually enjoy the back-and-forth. "I wasn't that bad a math student, but I would always confuse dates in history," he said. "I loved romantic novels, but if you asked me who jumped over a puddle and when, I would be totally lost."

"That's how I feel about the census," said the man. "Like, how can a bunch of numbers be helpful?"

Harry, just then, took quick note of all of the instruments in the living room—horns, guitars, violins, and an electric keyboard in a corner. He was intrigued and asked if he could step in further. Suddenly, census taking was the furthest thing from Harry's mind.

A prolific gesturer, the man waved Harry forward. He said, "I have an upright piano, too, stashed in the dining room, and small woodwinds in my bedroom."

Harry, who had played clarinet and alto sax in high school and now guitar, found the information far more engaging than any numbers he was supposed to collect. "I was an English major only because of one teacher. I thought it was so cool that he wrote novels."

The man was lost in another thought. "I don't actually have children, so my instruments are my kids," he said. He went through his living room, and Harry followed to the kitchen. He opened his refrigerator and took out a bottle of white wine and two beers. "Which?"

Harry pointed to the wine and received a mug with Leonard Bernstein's face on it. The man took a glass showing Louis Armstrong in caricature, white handkerchief aglow.

"Cheers," the man said, "even though no one should sketch Louis as even mildly cartoonish. He was a trumpeting, singing, high-energy genius."

Harry drank and quickly decompressed. "I thought maybe I could write a novel, like my English teacher did, but it didn't go so well. Did you ever try?"

"Can't say that I have. Most people call me Ed, but I actually prefer my given name: Edison."

As Harry sat, *The Saturday Review*, smashed into the rear pocket of his shorts, fell to the floor. He snatched at it and missed, getting it on the second try. Anticipating a question, Harry said, "It's the one with the intellectual article kind of damning The New Left. Also, a Dylan piece about his poetry and mysticism. Annoying stuff and exhilarating, too. I've been thinking, for the past month, about writing to

Dylan or that Irving Howe guy. Haven't gotten that thought out of my head and onto a page, though."

"Well said, Harry, I get your drift. With any good fortune, one day, all of a sudden, something unexpected happens," said Edison. He signaled for Harry to walk with him. Harry's curiosity was piqued.

Edison's bedroom was filled with more instruments, some houseplants, and one floor-to-ceiling bookshelf crammed with books. While some were vertically and others horizontally arranged, there was order to the configurations. Carefully situated index cards of different colors were placed upon a lengthy, wooden board that served as a desktop. Harry wandered over to look as Edison's lips soaked a reed for his clarinet.

"You must be a terrific teacher," said Harry.

Edison said, "Yes, I sub. But in this city, that often means work for quite a while. If someone's out and you're good and proficient, the replacement is not only valued but encouraged to stay on. Whatever I make is way less than money on a full-time line would be," he explained.

Harry had wanted to teach in a high school following his graduation from college, but he had procrastinated and missed the application deadlines. So, instead, he scrambled from one place to the next in a series of mostly forgettable jobs. He didn't last all that long as a Good Humor ice cream vendor. Busing restaurant tables in the hope of being promoted to waiter wasn't worth it. The exception was the summer camp after graduation. Teaching tennis to seven- and eight-year-olds was a gas. Harry, though, wanted to work with adolescents, thinking he had a much better feel for that age group.

He assumed Edison was called in as a sub for instrumental music, and that was partially true. Fill-ins for artistic subjects, however, were often asked to make or fake it through other genres. Ed couldn't paint worth a damn, but he knew how to take a picture.

Edison saw that Harry was intrigued with the instruments and obliged, on clarinet, with "Begin the Beguine." Seeing the look of delight on Harry's face, he said, "I have the RCA version with Artie Shaw doing that song, and I copied it. That's the way with musicians."

Smiling, Harry said, "I really, really wish I could do that. I mean, play that way. It's very impressive. Tell me how you reach teenagers."

Edison put down his clarinet and sat on the edge of his bed. Making a circle with his right index finger, he motioned for Harry to take the chair, sit in it, and face him. Then Edison snapped his fingers. "Connect," he quietly said. "If you get students on your side, you can do anything." He picked up a nearby guitar and sang, "When I left my home and my family, I was no more than a boy in the company of strangers in the quiet of the railway station, running scared . . ." Harry knew this was from Simon & Garfunkel's *Bridge Over Troubled Water* album, and he loved the lyrics. Edison extended a hand, which Harry grasped as the two sat next to each other.

Harry and his best friend, Sandy, had spent hours in college learning and then singing Simon & Garfunkel tunes. Sandy's voice rang true, while Harry, on a great day, could provide serviceable harmony. All good. The problem was that this particular song reminded Harry of Carolyn and their paused or lost love. Was there a chance it could still be found? Sandy was no longer, and Carolyn was, for now, gone. Why, Harry wondered, was he immersed in melancholy when he should be knocking on the door of his fifth or sixth apartment? Was Edison a diversion, or could he actually learn something here?

Just then, someone rapped hard on Edison's door, and Harry was amused to see Edison sprint to open it. A petite woman whose brown hair fell halfway down her back came in as if this was her place, too. She was that comfortable. She and Edison embraced warmly and closely. Harry did not especially wish for an intimate scene.

The woman backed off, smiled at Harry, and said, "I'm Lola, next apartment over. And you are?"

"Harry, a rookie census taker who should have come to your place a while ago. But Edison and his music kept me captive, and it's not easy to leave."

Edison laughed loudly and said to Lola, "Just when I had the kid wondering if you and I were, you know, having a thing."

"What, you think I'm easy?" Lola eyed Edison, who did not react, and then Harry, who shrugged.

"Easy is not the right adjective," Edison said. "Sweet. Maybe enticing."

Lola playfully jabbed Edison in the stomach. "Soft, not like when we first met," she said. "Even skinny guys can get fat. Watch your waistline."

"Lots of horn players sport their guts," said Edison. "Not me. I plan to do something about it."

"Sure, sugar," Lola said. "Hey, I came by for some eggs. You want some eggs, cutie?" she asked Harry. He hesitated, and Lola added, "Follow me. Lay four eggs on me, Ed, and I'll scramble them up for the boy."

Lola, escorting Harry, was at her kitchen stove, eggs in hand, within minutes. A dog nuzzled up to Harry, and then a pigtailed little girl, perhaps six or seven, came running at them. She saw Harry and forced a smile, which showed off her straight, bright upper row of teeth.

"Um, Lola, I need to ask you a few questions," said Harry. "Like who lives here—how many people?"

"Me, myself, and I," said Lola. "That's either three or one. This is my niece, Mel, and I'll be watching her for a couple of days. Would you mind including my dog if you're doing specific numbers?" she asked.

Harry knew that pets were not to be counted as household members, and Lola realized as much, too. "I think, handsome boy, that you should put down two," she said.

He nodded and wrote on his pad: "Question to myself—should I break the rules and put down the dog? I saw on the tag that its name is Murray."

Lola sidled up to Harry and said, "I can tell your mind is only half here. Love interest? I can see why.

If I weren't fifteen or twenty years older, I would definitely jump your bones. Except that you're too sweet for that." She flipped the eggs around a pan and divvied them up for all. Lola, crinkling her entire smiling face, raised the spatula in salute. The dog yelped, and Lola managed to shovel a bit into its mouth. Harry looked at Lola and grinned; he just could not help it. He was happy to once again be viewed as a kid. These people had lived for a while, and he was just emerging from a coming-of-age cocoon. Harry plopped himself down on a purple beanbag chair in a corner of Lola's kitchen.

She stepped behind him and massaged his neck and shoulders. "My God, you're stiff as an ironing board. Nice, but rigid," said Lola. Harry crumpled further into the beanbag.

Five years earlier, Harry had screamed for his independence. Now, he was open to admitting that some tender mothering was welcome. It wasn't fair to ask that of Carolyn, especially since they'd agreed to a timeout for reassessment. Lola's sure hands were therapeutic, and Harry could have stayed forever. The sudden revelation that he was very much still on the job jolted him to an upright position. "Lola," he said, "I need to get to the next apartment over. Who lives there?"

She grasped his hand securely, led him out of her place, walked him down the hallway, and tapped on the door one time before opening it. "Rosie, it's Lo. I got someone here you want to meet."

"Don't tell me she leaves her door unlocked," said Harry.

"The three of us kinda love like a bunch of hippies in a commune, if you catch my drift," she said.

Rosie, a large turquoise kerchief pressing her curly hair in place, grinned from ear to ear. She and Lola hugged, and then Lo pushed Harry further into Rosie's apartment.

"Where did you find this young one, Lo? Some catch," said Rosie.

"A sexy fox, yes he is," she replied, "and I think he has a sweetheart."

"Come in and sit. I have plenty of chocolate rugelach if you like," said Rosie.

Before he knew it, Harry was sitting between two warm, nurturing women who invited him into their conversation as if he had been part of the group for months. As they ate pastries and sipped coffee, Harry heard Rosie and Lo's family stories. Dogs were welcome in the apartment complex, and Harry heard barks emanating from a back room in Rosie's place and down the hall, too.

A dog named Henry ran into the dining room. Harry wondered how a dog could have such a name, as it happened to be so close to his own. Rosie explained that they were of Puerto Rican ancestry, so it would have been logical to name the dog Roberto after the baseball star, Roberto Clemente. But her husband was a Hank Aaron fan—hence the name Henry.

Harry knew he was a physical disaster. "Would you mind if I washed my face?" he asked. "I don't really know you, but you're both so nice. I can at least feel and maybe even look a little cleaner."

Rosie turned to Lola and said, "This boy was raised by good parents. He wants to spruce up for older women, which means us!" The two of them laughed, and Rosie pointed to the bathroom. "There are clean towels in the closet on the way in," she said. "You can even take a shower. Feel free."

Accepting the invitation, Harry lingered under the water for a while before emerging with a white towel wrapped around his middle. "Thank you for those few extra minutes," he said to Rosie, "and thanks to both of you for being friends."

"You're now our friend, too," said Lola.

"Where does Edison fit in?" Harry asked.

"A friendly teddy bear–type guy," said Rosie.

"He can also step up and become a big, protective brother whenever either of us needs him," added Lola.

Harry said, "He fooled me—seemed like a quirk a minute and then he was looking at me, through me, navigating my future for me. Know what I mean?"

Lola answered, "Ed helped me get through when I lost my husband who was in the shower when I heard a crash." She lifted both her arms. "He is gone forever. My son, Daniel, who is around your age, is out of the house now. It helps so much to have Rosie and Edison nearby."

Edison rumbled, unannounced, through Rosie's door. He carried with him a trombone and moved the slide back and forth, as if warming up for a performance. Anticipating Harry's question, he said, "I keep this under my bed. Shift from one to another. Trumpet was very early for me, and this baby is recent. I like to play around with it. The slide is total fun but also hard." He began to play "My Melancholy Baby." "It's a very neat fit for this instrument," he explained.

Edison then verbally injected a lyric line from the tune. "I love it, even though it's only a beginning of a thought. Feeling the music is the thing for me, paramount even when I'm subbing in schools. It's so hard to get that—reach teenagers whose hormones completely dominate."

Rosie interrupted, "Hot-blooded people like me, we hear music and have to move to it."

"I played clarinet and, luckily, sax, too, in high school," said Harry. "Pushed and stumbled into a jazz band, and that turned out to be the coolest. We played songs from the 30s and 40s. It was the only place where I was encouraged and not pressured, and it worked. What was, at first, fun became rewarding since I acquired some skills. So it was good for me and the band. For once, I wasn't just a very bright misfit. Learning to play in a jazz band taught me how to bend a little, give and take—just like the notes."

"Solitary and group: Both need to happen," said Edison. "Like I said, these instruments are like kids for me. Maybe I'm fooling myself, but I think I can bring these instruments to young people who may be seeking compassion. Think about the wistfulness of the cello. I also have a flute and piccolo, both of which I'm now learning. For me, it is about levity and joie de vivre."

When Edison talked music, he lit up. Every crease of his face, his fingertips—all exuded emotion. The man filled the room with feelings even when not playing—ever conducting. Rosie saw him eye her small spinet piano in the corner of the dining room. He dashed to it and began to play Paul McCartney's "Yesterday." Swaying to his rendition, he encouraged everyone in the room to sing; before long, they were all improvising, bending words to suit the occasion.

The lyrics, though, sent Harry's thoughts back to May and the bloodshed at Kent State. He and Sandy and others were sure they would change the world, fix it. Seemingly in a flash, Sandy was gone, then students slain on a college campus. His eyes filled with tears.

"Querida, Harry, dear boy, what is it?" asked Rosie. "Querida is a way of referring to a girlfriend. You miss someone you love?"

Harry didn't know whether or how to tell these warmhearted people he'd just met that yes, it was a love interest on his mind—but much more, too. He was consumed with darkness and death. Rosie interrupted that daytime nightmare by telling him the story of her youth—when she and her sisters and parents were stuffed into a few rooms. She couldn't recall whether anything like census had been taken in Puerto Rico.

Harry continued to question his motives, his life. He was expected to visit at least twenty apartments today, and he had only been to three. He was broke, and he couldn't motivate himself to get up. Instead, he thought about The Beatles and Simon & Garfunkel. Everything, at that very moment, was soulful. He, himself, was running and he was scared, but Harry did not want to leave these new friends.

❧ ❧

The next morning, Rosie wedged open her apartment door and both Edison and Lola came in to find Harry there. Richard had arrived from his night shift quite early and, seeing Harry, awakened Rosie who quickly filled him in.

"Yeah, I got the cute boy who wants his cute girl with him," said Rosie. "He does this census thing because he needs money."

Harry was wearing a fresh T-shirt, this one with a New York Knicks logo on the front. "Breakfast together is regular here?" he asked.

Everyone nodded. "If you could have one thing, kid, what would that be?" Edison asked.

Harry liked to hide under the "dreamer" umbrella when possible but thought he ought to answer the question.

Before he did, though, Lola was saying just how young he looked, peach fuzz on his chin and all.

"Boston. I would say going to Boston is what I want," said Harry.

"Even though it's half of what New York is, I like it there—for one day," Edison said.

Harry went on with his thoughts about how New York was too much, too good. If New York City was a giant lake, Boston was, in comparison, a pond.

He still wanted to get there, but, of course, that involved Carolyn, for whom he was pining away. He knew that he could land on the couch at a good friend's place on Massachusetts Avenue. On the other hand, this—the census taking—was what Sandy and he had agreed to do. So Harry felt a pull to follow through with it for him. Harry still could not believe that Sandy had been left to die in a hit-and-run. He didn't do well with the death: skipped the funeral, had his own private moment with Sandy elsewhere. Now, these three strangers were taking him in—a messed-up kid who was getting more confused by the minute.

"Baby, tell us more," said Lola. "You're hurting since you lost your best brother kind of friend. And you really haven't talked about the girl. I mean, I want people around me because I'm really missing someone, too. My son, Daniel, was the joy of my life. He's probably your age, turning twenty-three soon. He took care of us all after my husband died. I just heard a smashing noise coming from the shower more than two years ago—massive heart attack, and it was over."

Rosie followed by talking about her husband, Richard, whom she adored. The problem was that he worked from midnight till 7:00 a.m. and then slept. Their kids were in school or camp, leaving her all alone most of the time. "It's hard," she said, this ebullient soul who was perpetually smiling.

"Me, it's about my own music and a handful of special students," said Edison. "I take care of my instruments as if they're humans: A guitar or a horn speaks to me when I play it. Many grown-ups—I don't know. It's safer to be friends with a violin or piano." He went on to talk about tuning a Steinway and the satisfaction he derived when a consummate musician played a sonata on it.

Having taken keyboard lessons in college, Harry understood. He was adept with chords and improvisation—less so as a note reader. He was reluctant, sometimes, to sit in or play with others. And soloing. He immediately hoped that Edison could get him motivated and sharpen his skills.

Edison immediately stood and walked out of the apartment.

"What did I say?" asked Harry.

"He moves on impulse," Rosie explained. "I bet he comes back with at least one instrument."

"Plus a harmonica in his pocket," said Lola. "This keeps him happy, drives away the blues."

Edison returned, predictably, with a guitar that appeared handmade, such was its exquisite design. The surprise was that he carried a small keyboard under his arm.

"Harry, this is for you," he said as he gave him the keyboard. "Try 'Sweet Baby James' with E, A, D, G, B, E. You can do this." Edison started to hum and sing the melody and accompanied himself on guitar.

Harry fiddled with the keyboard before finding the power button. He played E and A chords and glanced at the two women, both of whom were smiling. Pleased, Harry asked Edison if they could try. By the last line, Edison was familiar with Harry's voice and added sweet harmony.

Lola had edged forward to fully appreciate the impromptu performance. "I am so sure you love that girl, the one who is almost gone," she said to Harry. I mean, for me to lose Jack which was heartbreaking."

"You two know that dogs are safer. I live by myself, yeah," said Edison. "I've tried to be with someone, but it's better solo."

Until now, Rosie had been silent as she took it all in. She turned to Edison and said, "Ed, you don't have kids. Always, though, it seems Lola's family is around her. Me? Well, it sometimes is a struggle but surviving, yes. On the rare times when Richard and I happen to be here together, given schedules, we can peer into each other's face and see both the love and the stress, too. The little ones look like us, so we can live through them. I imagine a day when they lead us. I can really see this."

Harry realized he was having trouble disciplining himself to do his job, to take census. He could not wait for Saturday off. He also acknowledged that he was distracted. Sure, missing Carolyn—but more than that.

"I can't get out of my own way," he said to anyone in the room who would listen. "You know, my future was wide open and then all of a sudden death takes over. My friend and then the blood of kids my own age on TV. I lose my breath even thinking about that."

Rosie took his hand and brought it up to her eyes to look at it. She put her palm to his forehead. "That is why we have the word loss," she said. "You are immediately limited, constrained, and confused. I know."

Edison held his guitar up and matched that with a thumbs-up.

The mood livened with the acute high pitch of a dog's bark at the door. Lola and Rosie simultaneously let in a scampering black and white pooch, a dog who seemed to smile.

"Man, if only they lived fifty or sixty years," said Rosie. "Please, everyone, follow me and sit. I will bring pancakes and coffee." She walked away as people settled around the table. Quickly returning with a tray, she added, "I assume everyone wants coffee, including the boy?" The cups she distributed were solid red, orange, green, blue, and purple. "I do the color wheel. Remember where I'm from: Puerto Rico, where the flag is red, white, and blue but not exactly like the United States's. White is too basic a color for me, and that is why I choose gold. Music people, come on and let's sing 'Here Comes the Sun.'"

Harry was, once again, relieved that one of these new friends was able to release him from his funk. When Lola asked him about Carolyn, he was forthcoming, told them she was supposed to go to graduate school at Tufts, near Boston.

"Get yourself to that couch in Cambridge, boy," said Edison. "You cannot predict the future."

Harry's thoughts flew to Carolyn. He could do that—go look for her—and then what? He was certain the drama would resume: They'd decide to be together forever, but then either he or Carolyn would nerve out. And who really wants to be hurt or hurt anyone else? They were two hypersensitive souls trying to find the perfect balance between intimacy and freedom, which was, of course, impossible. Yeah, he could be generous and caring but also, within a nanosecond, self-indulgent. Well, maybe that was harsh. Better to say looking out for himself. Or, Harry knew he could stay where he was, make it through the weekend, take census all day Monday and Tuesday, not give up on this whole thing before even really trying. He knew he was not, by nature, a lingerer. Really, though, judging this gig without giving it a shot made no sense. He did have a place to stay and, in theory, could make some money if he would just go door to door. Not to mention he now had these cool friends who instantly seemed to both like and accept him. Going to Boston meant no job and only a maybe, not a guarantee, when it came to Carolyn. Harry decided to other older, and probably wiser, people in the room what they thought.

"If I just go for that and follow my heart, I could lose out," said Harry, shaking his head from side to side.

Edison pointed at his stomach and then Harry's. "The seat of your emotions, the middle of your body," Edison said. "It's where we find enough breath to play trumpet, where a good actor gets his wind and voice for projection."

Harry looked at the women in the room. They joined hands and pointed to their hearts.

Rosie said, "Edison meant this, too."

Lola added, "You gotta have plenty of heart. Really, and what Ed said."

At that very moment, Harry wished that maybe he hadn't been such a model child: a goody-goody. He knew he couldn't quit the job even if he wanted to. He could hear one of his parents (he wasn't even sure which one) advising him to stick it out. He used this thought as a catalyst to force himself from the comfort of these seasoned people who seemingly wanted him as a fourth for their group.

Before he could change his mind, Harry said, "I need to do more census taking today before I totally blow off this chance. How about we talk later?"

"Lunch here on Monday," said Rosie.

"You are just too cute," said Lola to Harry. "And before you tell me no one ever said that to you, just that you were interesting looking, here's my advice again: Go to that girl. You want her."

Chapter 2

Cambridge,

Briefly

HARRY SAT ON A tattered rug, his legs beneath a rickety wooden coffee table in the living room of a ramshackle apartment. After a couple of weeks taking census, he had left the city for his friend's place in Cambridge, just outside of Boston. The place was no great shakes, filled with clutter that included dirty laundry, a few stacks of records, and a multitude of books. Still, Harry liked the camaraderie—that other people lived in this cramped space, that this was a post-college scene in an Ivy League college town. Massachusetts Avenue connected Cambridge with Boston, and cars were constantly rumbling by just outside the front door.

He thought about the past month. The census taking job did get better as he became more familiar with the neighborhood and more proficient at gathering and entering data. Each day he wasn't with them, though, he missed Edison, Rosie, and Lola.

Then came the trip to Boston. He hadn't seen Carolyn in months, but he still hoped that she would become his girlfriend—again.

Harry had been scared ever since he had called her the day before, when he arrived. He felt she was out of his league; she was so electrifying. Men stared at her, and he once heard someone passing by say, "You're drop-dead gorgeous." She had blushed that time, but he had also seen her become furious at the thought of being viewed as an object. It was right that they had turned down the temperature on the relationship, but he still wanted her. The time away did, for him, make both his heart and body grow fonder. He was antsy waiting for her to get there in the car she had borrowed. He loved the contours of her body.

The doorbell issued forth a couple of chimes when she rang it. He looked out and first saw her dark brown hair with the highlighted golden streaks flowing down her back. She wore a Red Sox cap and sunglasses. When he opened the door, she leapt into his waiting arms and said, "My God, I cannot believe how much I've missed you."

"Me, too," answered Harry. "Maybe we should get married." He squeezed her more tightly, pulling her into the apartment.

"What? Sure. You're totally crazy. I don't know how to do that, where to go. Justice of the peace? I've watched movies," said Carolyn. "I mean, I have a dress, but I doubt you have a suit. And how would our parents react?"

"I think I was kidding, but I don't know," Harry said, pulling Carolyn to the couch. For weeks, this had been the dream, just touching her again, and he wasn't about to let go. "This is probably my section of this sofa—I can't really even claim a corner—but I'm here for you. The Lower East Side was complicated."

He then launched into a narrative about Edison, Rosie, and Lola. He told Carolyn all about these people who had become his instant friends. Carolyn wanted to meet them, so Harry told her it was "not if but when." He went on about being taken in, taken care of by perfect strangers. Carolyn asked whether they would be married before she met them. That stopped him.

❧❧❧❧❧ ❧❧❧❧❧

At that very moment, Edison, Rosie, and Lola were talking about Harry. Midway through the afternoon wine and cheese at her apartment, Rosie blurted out, "He's so sweet and innocent, I just wanted to spare him pain."

"We're really not the kid's parents," said Edison.

Lola interrupted, "But he's young and, well, women might understand better, Edison. You're a beautiful guy, but you relate to your guitar, trumpet, and electric piano."

"When it comes to philosophy, Edison, you got something now but when you were twenty-two?" Rosie asked. "That boy is smart, and he was doing a job. We need to call him."

Lola explained that when Harry first came to her place, he had given her a confirmation paper indicating that he was really a census taker. She didn't know where it was. Rosie had her copy, and she thought there was a phone number at the bottom of the page. They agreed to call it even if Edison suspected they might find one of Harry's parents on the other end. Then they hugged one another.

"I say he's a part of our little tribe and we're not letting go of him," said Rosie.

Harry was wondering if his trio of friends would support this crazy idea of marrying Carolyn. As he tried to sort it out, Carolyn suggested it might be easier to live together. "A tryout," she said, "so that we can avoid the marriage forever thing for maybe a little while. You're the one who always says contracts are just pieces of paper."

Feeling bombarded and confused, Harry told Carolyn that the friend he was staying with had mentioned that there was a vacant apartment upstairs. "I have no idea what it looks like. I mean, I can have this couch corner, but after four or five days, that would get old. I would have to contribute, and I don't have a job."

"Harry, we're still kids and the picture you're painting is of this married couple maybe renting a place? How do we support that? I work part time, and you left after a few weeks, census boy."

"Uh huh. Still, quit your job and let's go to New York. These people already love you and they've never even met you."

New York City—again

A week later, Carolyn and Harry sat at either end of a big room. He tried to stabilize a small, rickety bookshelf, and she pulled a bedspread embossed with multicolored flowers over a worn and weary sofa. Each of them was, nevertheless, smiling.

He, at last, balanced the makeshift wooden shelves, but after a moment, the contraption toppled. Harry said, "At least we don't have many books."

"I know," said Carolyn. "We don't have many anything." She stopped and looked directly at him. "You don't really look like a Harry, never did. I mean, that's a name for someone over fifty. It's so formal, as in Houdini or, better than that, Truman. Yeah, Harry Truman, a president they sorta skipped over in our high school history book."

"Who knows why they named me Harry? The only one I know about and kind of like is Belafonte. My older cousin had all his 1950s albums. Every time I went to see him, he would play the 'Banana Boat Song'—things like that. I mean, at that time I thought it was kind of terrific. And Harry Agganis, a baseball player who died young. I was such a baseball dork and what I remember is that he was on the Red Sox and all of a sudden died of something."

Carolyn couldn't resist him when he acted like a ten- or twelve-year-old. She slid right into Harry, pressed her body against his. "Love that about you when you put together calypso with baseball. Too cute."

"Well, I am glad, but we still have nothing. I like both of your names: Carolyn and Carrie," he said.

She sighed, "'Harry and Carrie' is like what I would put on the cover of a loose-leaf notebook when I was in sixth grade."

He began to laugh as he got up and said, "I'm getting some boxes from the hallway. Will you love me when I'm thirty-eight and maybe losing hair and gaining weight?"

"Anyone else would pick forty. What if I said I would still be in love with you at thirty-eight but not by the time you hit forty?"

"You're one to talk about numbers. When we did that forced split-up, you wanted seven weeks. Like, because of the Bible stuff—seven days? Or a lucky number, Carolyn?" Harry awkwardly hoisted the carton, while Carolyn explained that since God rested on the seventh day, that one would be ideal for coming back together. Harry showed the large card pasted on the box, which read "Dear Harry and Carolyn, here are some practical items you might need. We love you both—our son and his girl. Mom and Dad."

Harry reached inside and lifted an iron as he shrugged his shoulders.

"Maybe one of us gets a job that requires good clothes, like wrinkle-free," he said.

Carolyn reached her hand deeply into the box and withdrew a toothbrush holder. "The problem is I'm so attracted to you, but when I think about being a couple forever, that just seems both too soon and too weird," she said.

Harry took the toothbrush holder and started fiddling with it. "I guess this thing actually holds two so, again, it's for married people? Anyway, so for whatever reason you liked the way I looked and that made you go for a hiatus?"

Carolyn nodded and added that her father pushed her to be sure she married someone with whom she could imagine growing old—and she wasn't one hundred percent certain it was Harry. She then dropped her hand into the box and came up with a rabbit's foot.

Harry's face lit up. "I found that at the beach just as the ocean was about to swallow it up. I grabbed it as a wave smacked me, and I thought that was the end: total obliteration. I put it on the desk in my room like six or seven years ago, and here it is. My folks probably think it's a good luck charm," he said.

Lost in thought recalling her father's advice, Carolyn was half listening to Harry and then said, "Maybe he was right, so what about we think about when we're sixty-eight instead of thirty-eight? Let's say this works out and we even have kids." She talked about what it was like in Boston trying to fly solo for a while, putting one foot in front of the other, the mundane ritual of it all. "Then you said you were coming. I'm hoping we can just survive here in New York. I don't know about this crystal ball stuff."

"Tomorrowland at the World's Fair. I can't imagine what the world will look like in the year 2000," said Harry. "I mean, phones with pictures?" As he rolled his eyes, something crashed loudly beneath them. "Jesus, what was that?"

"Your friends are just a floor down, and that's where it came from," said Carolyn. With that, Harry grabbed her hand and the pair ran out of their newly rented apartment and down a staircase before stopping at Rosie's place. Harry rapped on the door repeatedly. She quickly ushered them in, then remarked that Harry and Carolyn were too sweet for having the same color hair and that Harry's was nearly as long as Carolyn's.

"We came because of the blast. You, okay?" asked Harry as Rosie put her mouth to a wall and yelled for Lola.

"Yeah, that must have scared the crap out of you. Lola's oven exploded!" she said, laughing.

Lola rushed in, apologized to everyone, and then said it wasn't the first time. "A lemon since I bought it," she explained in reference to the villainous oven. "Sorry, kids."

Harry said, "Is that what an earthquake sounds like?"

Before he could continue, Carolyn cut him off. "Stop it," she said. "Nothing moved. We don't know anyone on the floors above us. Just you guys and Edison."

Whereupon Edison joined the group and advised that the noise was minor, a "little pfff."

"I could understand it if a car backfired next to you," he continued.

Lola and Rosie erupted when they heard "pfff."

Harry wanted to know if anybody in the room had married young.

"I did," said Lola. "I met Jack when I was eighteen. He was two years older. I was just graduating from high school and felt like he had already experienced the big, bad world. The physical part we were the same—hungry every single minute for each other. We drank a lot of wine, which was probably not the greatest thing to do. If we kept it up, we would have become alcoholics. As it was, I couldn't fit into my clothes. No one told me that wine made you fat. One night, when we were naked, we just decided to get married and we did. Sorry for the ramble, but I guess it's exciting to even say that much. We really didn't think about it a whole lot."

Edison shook his head from side to side indicating that he had not indulged in marriage.

Rosie explained that she and Richard had dated forever, then gotten engaged and had a big wedding. They then had kids nearly three apart. "Henry, the dog, is the prince of the family," she said. "He's adopted, but now he's forever, too."

"Your lady friend is completely gorgeous, Harry," said Lola. "Rosie and me, we knew you were head over heels for her, and I can see why."

Rosie added, "For a shaggy-haired kid, you're not so bad, either. I know we're not supposed to go by looks."

Before she knew it, Carolyn was singing from *Guys and Dolls* and then she took off on a tangent of her own.

Edison clapped and said, "My God, you can sing."

Carolyn and Harry explained that while they went to different high schools, each was in a production of *Oklahoma!* Both still knew the score, and Harry added, "She has the heavenly voice to get us through a duet."

"I told you," said Lola.

"I know they're a perfect fit," added Rosie as Lola nodded.

"Just trying to figure it out," said Harry. His father had advised him to see the world—play the field, as the cliché went—while Carolyn's parents counseled not to jump at the first guy. She explained that her mother almost did just that. Rosie then offered up her apartment as a place for the wedding.

Harry smiled but said, "I think we'll stick to singing for now. That would be fun and maybe, Edison, you could help us out. If we come to your place, could you give us some pointers? Just do whatever works for your students?"

"Sure thing. Tomorrow morning?"

Edison had opened all the windows allowing for a breeze and now sat at the piano to explain that the piece was one in progress. Then he motioned for Harry and Carolyn to stand on either side of him and face Rosie and Lola, who were seated on the tattered dark red Persian rug. He played an introduction, raised his left hand toward the performers, and together they sang lines from "People Will Say We're in Love."

Silence. And then Rosie simply said, "Oh, my."

Lola chimed in: "Way too much romance for the morning. It almost makes me dizzy, but I needed a good reason to swoon, to laugh, you know?"

Carolyn claimed Harry had dragged her to Washington Square Park, but he interrupted and said, "Hardly dragging. I just thought it would be kind of cool to practice the song there. You never know what exactly will happen, who will show up. You could get hit by a flying Frisbee while you're dancing. Maybe just hang out and watch guys playing chess all day long. It sort of worked out to be there."

Rosie talked about the rare occasions, mostly on Sundays, when she and Richard were on the same schedule. They would take the kids just so they could look at people. "We tell them it's not polite to stare. Yeah. I mean, they're boys who are six and eight and a half. They might fight with each other, but when they're out in the world together, they form this wall. Don't mess with them. That's when they really stick together and stand up for the other one. Otherwise, not so much."

"I saw Allen Ginsberg there when he was leading a snake dance with the accordion guy," Lola said. "Allen and Peter. It's definitely a cross between meditation and a story."

The anecdote roused Edison, who played a chord on the piano and said, "I was out there one time with Ginsberg and Orlovsky. I wish I could recall the name of the school where I was subbing. Dammit, where was that? They had a ramshackle auditorium that doubled as a gym. Everyone's just sitting there, and this long-haired string bean of an English teacher comes out and says they have special guests. One is wearing a dark suit and a tie, but the other has multicolored shawls over his shoulders. Ginsberg says a few things and then asks if anyone wants to play recorder as they chant. It was right up my alley, so I did it. The entire place fell under a trance. I've never seen anything like it—a spell. Man, the thrill of playing with those two."

Harry knew about Ginsberg through "Howl" and "Kaddish," which he experienced through a school-within-the-high-school creative workshop. He did not know that Orlovsky was Ginsberg's partner. Lola found Ginsberg charismatic, and she thought he was proud of his Judaism, whatever version it was. She wondered about his coupling with Orlovsky, who didn't seem a match. And Rosie had seen him in the neighborhood when he was around. She knew that he also spent time in San Francisco, and she'd been intrigued with the whole Beat Poet and Fiction scene, what with Kerouac and Burroughs. She talked of watching Ginsberg read with Gregory Corso and wondered how Ginsberg could be a Jew and then a Buddhist.

Edison changed the mood and topic by asking Carolyn to sing.

She immediately nodded and said to Edison, at the keyboard, "Soon It's Gonna Rain." He supplied a quick intro before she performed as if auditioning. Harry joined in for the last lines of the tune.

Edison, enthralled, asked if they both had done that show, *The Fantasticks*, too. Harry replied that he and Carolyn had seen it at Sullivan Street in the Village.

Carolyn elaborated by calling it a "big date," then quickly added, "even though we were careful at that time not to call it a date. We loved it so much we found a shop nearby to get the cast album right away. Now it has a home in our apartment. I'm amazed that our voices are compatible. I guess that's lucky."

At that point, Lola dubbed them lovebirds and Edison referred to them as love-struck teenagers, but Rosie pointed out that they were not teens.

"It does look like you've been together for a while," said Edison. "You move together, if you know what I mean." He looked around the room for agreement and then continued, "I was close to being married once, but things were not exactly right. We never sang in harmony, if you know what I mean. Besides, look at the way I live." He talked about his apartment and the confines of it, which he argued were perfect for a single person, "especially with all of my musical friends as occupants: conga drums, bells, all of the horns, you know."

"I just like doing songs with Carolyn because it draws us together even if we're in the middle of a disagreement," Harry said. "Not the crazy, loud rock tunes, but The Beatles or The Mamas & the Papas or The Byrds. I happen to like doing harmony on 'Sweet Baby James,' maybe because I'm better on that than lead."

Harry and Carolyn knew that James Taylor was twenty-two or twenty-three, and both of them liked to think of him as a contemporary.

Edison said, "I don't know if you're ready to be married, but you can definitely perform." He paused and looked at the young people. "Plenty of small places have nights welcoming new singers. You're way better than many I've seen. Can we go back to the romantic song, the one from *Oklahoma!*? I remember key signatures, but not names. This one, for just the intro, key of G and then C."

Carolyn and Harry launched themselves into it, easily recalling the lyrics.

"Oh, my God," said Rosie as Lola gave a thumbs-up.

Harry and Carolyn again leaned into one another as Rosie and Lola beamed and Edison ran his fingers across his keyboard. Then he said, "That never happens for me. I get hugs for playing, or people say things like, 'Without you, we're nothing.' Stuff like that." He ran his fingers through his hair. "But, you know, instead of trying for an evening out somewhere, we could perform right here. We have an audience: Rosie and Lola, and maybe Rosie's kids and whoever Lola has around. Everyone who shows up she says is a cousin. Is it too lame to perform for some friends or get together a solo gig which could reinvent hours later for Richard?

Carolyn and Harry agreed that singing for people they knew was easier than performing for strangers at a club. Edison added that it was not necessarily an either-or. After a warm-up session, they could keep practicing and maybe, he suggested, get to a place like Gerde's. Harry thought that a prime place like that was out of reach, but he was willing to try. Carolyn laughed.

"Okay, so we go away and you guys practice," Lola said. "See you later, like at 4:00. Ro, your apartment is better, but what about the kids?" She answered her own question: "We'll get one of the teens in the building to look after them. Let's meet at my apartment."

It occurred to Harry that his higher priority should be looking for a job. When he mentioned that, Rosie told him that it was okay to keep the arts on a front burner. She urged him to think of it as preparing for the 24 East Houston Street talent show. Even dogs and a stray cat were welcome. Carolyn took Harry's hand, said they needed to go, and dragged him through the hallway and up the staircase. She just said, "Come on."

⁂

Back in their own place, Harry and Carolyn held hands, kissed again, and agreed that they enjoyed spending time with all three of their downstairs neighbors. With sealed cartons thrown about, they decided that they probably would survive. When Carolyn noted that no one had to sleep on a living room couch, Harry asked, "You call this a couch?"

She did not answer but remarked, "We're just two kids who are barely out of college, and we need money." Harry told her that he would have something by the end of September and that would get them through. If things became worse, he could work for the highway department where he grew up. She raised her eyebrows, and he said, "I read that in fancy suburbs you can actually make a small living doing that."

Carolyn said, "But we just moved into an apartment on the Lower East Side. We are trying to make it here, right? Without robbing a bank or robbing one and not getting caught?"

Harry loved the comment. "We say it together—you know, like Virgil in *Take the Money and Run*, who cannot spell gun so he ends up in the slammer."

They embraced once again, and Carolyn said, "

Sounds like us, don't you think?"

Soon they were reminiscing about childhood: lemonade stands and treats. They thought of the upcoming "performance" and agreed that, at the very least, Rosie's and Lola's desserts would make the whole thing worth it. Finally, Carolyn admitted that she no longer felt like a teenager, which brought Harry back to the reality of seeking employment.

He said, "Look at Edison. He's kind of part boy and part grown-up, don't you think? Working with kids in schools, his music. . . it's as though he's extending college. That's the way I see it, and I find it amazing, really."

To which Carolyn replied, "Still not exactly my role model. Let's go get him."

With that, they walked quickly down the hall, took the stairs, and moments later were rapping on Edison's door. He opened it, and they got a quick glimpse of a man somewhere in middle age wearing an NYU sweatshirt and striped Bermuda shorts but no shoes.

Edison said, "You don't have to beat down the door. Here for lunch?" Carolyn apologized for barging in while he was not fully dressed, but Edison interrupted her. "Actually, Carolyn, I prefer bare feet." He was careful to enunciate the three syllables of her name: "Car-o-lyn."

Harry asked what the plan for the music might be. Edison said the three of them would work together to come up with something. He added, "I knew you two would take the bait, but getting here in less than an hour tells me a great deal. You're probably still a bit in the dark. It's best to come in with something everyone knows and give it a spin, or else bring an original. And I know how to do that. All you have to do is tell me what it's like to be under twenty-five and entangled all of the time, and I'll come up with the beginning of a song."

Harry nodded as Carolyn asked, "Is it possible to sing 'Love Me Tender' in two-part harmony?"

Explaining that he was just old enough to have been an Elvis fan in the 1950s, Edison sat at the piano, mentioned he first learned the song on guitar, and said, "Just an F sharp so key of G." He began to play and asked, "You know the lyrics?" Failing to rouse a response, he sang solo and added, "Carolyn, you take the second line. I know it by heart."

"Okay," she said. Harry soon joined in, followed by Edison. They sang together as if they had been practicing it forever.

No one uttered a sound until Edison exploded with, "Fantastic! Now, Carolyn, lower register alto. And Harry, can you go a bit higher? Make it happen, lovebirds. Swoon. Do the first sequence."

Harry and Carolyn obliged. At first, Carolyn took the melody line, then both harmonized at the end.

Edison jumped up and brought them together to join hands, as if they were basketball players during a timeout. "That's it, what you did—that final harmony. You each have more than enough range to switch high and low. And in the beginning, allow room to grow, so to speak. I can play a third voice behind you; I can try that. I have this old reel-to-reel tape recorder. We can sample that idea. You guys are the main act, and I'm the happy piano player or guitarist."

Harry and Carolyn wondered if one song was enough, which prompted further response from Edison: "Everyone pretty much dismissed the 1950s. People drop back to the 40s for tunes. It seems to me that we should try a song called 'My Special Angel,' but I don't want you totally turned off by the title."

Harry explained, "I was a pretty decent kid but never an angel."

Edison went on about the special quality of the decade even as he acknowledged that everyone was pretending during those years. "The war was over, and either you had what you wanted or said that you did. This is a romantic love song about innocence."

Still, Carolyn wasn't certain she could sing a song about an angel—it was too much of a stereotype. Edison explained it was a man singing and a woman harmonizing. "Here, listen: 'You are my special angel, sent from up above. The Lord smiled down on me and sent an angel to love.'"

"Come on, Edison. I'm really going to sing those words?" asked Harry.

"It's not so bad to sing about an angel coming down to spread love," he replied.

"My God, your chords are beautiful, Edison," said Carolyn.

Inspired, Edison launched into a prolific keyboard introduction and then sang the beginning of the song before ushering in Harry and Carolyn.

No one said a word for a minute or two before Harry asked, "Anything else we need to go over? I mean, it is beautiful and romantic, but I have to get a job. Maybe we both do. For money."

Edison was still immersed in the music. He agreed that singing for just Lola and Rosie would be perfect for now, and he hoped for an honest response. If he read it as genuinely positive, perhaps a church would be next.

Carolyn agreed with Edison, thinking that limiting the audience to Rosie and Lola first would be perfect. She also knew that Harry was right to think that they wouldn't be able to live upstairs if they couldn't find work. Harry thought there might be some extra census work still available since, for some reason, they seemed to like him, even though he clearly did not do the job. Carolyn wanted to go with him when Harry went back to see if they could use him. She said, "I can help even by tagging along. Besides, I'm better meeting total strangers than you are."

"You're certainly prettier," he replied.

Edison held his focus on the music: "'Turn! Turn! Turn!' like the way The Byrds recorded it. The exquisite blend of your voices will be sensational, and there might even be room enough for me to sing into that one." As he spoke, Edison played an introduction while Harry and Carolyn stepped up to sing together the lyrics about laughing, weeping, and healing.

They were interrupted by rapid knocks on Edison's front door and a quick entrance by Rosie and Lola, who explained that the walls remained thin. Rosie added that they could always hear Edison playing. She carried a plate filled with chocolate chip cookies. Saying he needed to eat, Edison grabbed them and Lola playfully poked his little belly.

Rosie said she thought they sounded different from The Byrds but just as good. Harry explained his parents' love for Pete Seeger; he had first heard the song on one of their records. Carolyn admitted to having a crush on Roger McGuinn, the Byrds' vocalist. She turned to Harry to assure him that McGuinn wasn't a threat to him.

Next, Edison led into Paul McCartney's "Yesterday," swaying but not singing to his rendition. He did not need to stop to ask his young friends to contribute their voices—they knew to do so.

"Sublime," said Edison. "Can you play guitar?" he asked Carolyn, who took one of Edison's guitars as Lola asked her to hold hands with Harry. Lola wanted to gauge a picture, then added that photography was her hobby. She urged them to lean into one another, not be shy. Edison said, "You do that, Lo; I want the girl's voice. I just get excited when someone is on pitch that way. Sorry."

Harry said, "I used to be able to really sing. Now, passable does fine. When Car and I were in Boston, we would spend evenings singing show tunes and folk music."

Carolyn had had eyes for Harry ever since the two had attended the same two-week arts camp the summer after junior year of high school. The boy was always disheveled, sometimes sweaty, never quite put together, and, for her, a sexual lure. She had to be the aggressor since he seemed more interested in sports and music than girls. The workshop instructor brought them together for the first time when she assigned them roles as Hamlet and Ophelia in an exercise. That was the start, but it was Mrs. Columbus's follow-up that served as the coupling device Carolyn wanted. Mrs. C asked them to imagine that the play was set in contemporary times. "Breathe new life into the tragedy of these teenagers," she said. "Somehow or other, they need to be survivors." The teacher challenged them to meet and write another scene, keeping her instructions in mind. She said if one scene was going well, do more; write a one-act play. If that went well . . .

After sharing this memory with the group, Carolyn said, "Anyway, we have this memorized. Right, Harry?" When Harry nodded, she said, "Here it goes."

Hamlet: Let's elope.

Ophelia: Where to?

Hamlet: I'm not sure. Also, what else are we supposed to do?

Ophelia: Ham, get with the program. It might mean buying a suit and a dress.

Hamlet: I thought the point of eloping was to escape and be alone together.

Ophelia: Even so, I always thought when I got married, I would look my best.

Hamlet: Hey, but aren't we supposed to be star-crossed? By the way, what does that actually mean?

Ophelia: If we could travel back to when this was written, we could get a meeting and ask the author. I once did research on him and read that Will Shakespeare was a distant person. That's a nice way of saying he had no warmth. Also, someone reported that if he was talking to you, he would look over your shoulder instead of focusing on your eyes.

Hamlet: What a charmer. The guy who created both of us and what we're doing here was quite an actor, too.

Ophelia: I really don't know if he was gifted on stage, but when I looked into him, it became clear that he knew about money. He was pretty rich by the time he died.

Hamlet: Look at me—I'm a brooding person who might be doing some seriously intense therapy. Will just had to understand human emotions to paint me with deep blue colors, if you know what I mean.

Ophelia: I go crazy. (Sighs.) In some other plays, though, Shakespeare is totally laugh-out-loud funny. Couldn't he have given me even a hint of that? I'm an infatuated, maybe sexy adolescent who is also heartbroken. (Pauses.) Is there a way to go back to Carolyn and Harry and keep writing? I love Mrs. C's read, but I want to write, well, from me.

Hamlet: She wants us to be these characters.

Ophelia: Keep writing in their voices.

Hamlet: Can we do something more
than talk?

Ophelia: I think I know where you're
going with that, and it's not about
dancing.

With that, Harry and Carolyn turned to Rosie,
Lola, and Edison and bowed. The audience of
three clapped and whooped as loudly as possible.

"Wow!" said Rosie.

"Give us a couple of days to practice," Harry
added.

"I hope with me, too," said Edison. "Definitely
with me, too."

❧❧❧❧❧ ❧❧❧❧❧

It was late morning, two days after, that the entire
contingent, including two dogs who were totally
comfortable with each other, gathered at Edison's
place. He had moved the electric piano to the living room. Ed's idea of hospitality meant an open
a package of Ritz crackers, a bottle of rosé, and a
wedge of cheddar cheese. Lola brought in colorful
paper napkins and plates, while Rosie furnished
variously designed plastic glasses. Harry wore clean
pants and a plain maroon T-shirt. Carolyn's jeans

were embroidered with flowers and she chose a Joni Mitchell–style top.

Edison, sitting at the keyboard, explained that they had practiced for about forty minutes the day before. He proclaimed them ready, then began the melody, and raised his eyebrows at Harry and Carolyn, who sang with harmony a resonant version of "People Will Say We're in Love." Harry added that they'd not yet worked on anything more than the first verse, which he and Carolyn recalled from their separate high school days.

Lola talked about how "the kids fit hand in glove." Rosie pitched in with, "On the other hand, they probably need to see each other's warts, if you know what I mean. Richard and I went through a couple of tricky patches."

Carolyn burst out with, "Harry's had this one wart on his left hand for how many years?"

"Okay," Harry responded, "so she doesn't have any warts, but I know about something else of hers."

Edison urged them back to the music by telling them that they could someday find an open mic after this promising start but that they needed to chase it. Harry wanted a few hours to get lunch with Carolyn. Then, they could all gather again at 2:00 or so. They agreed to reconvene at Edison's then. He reminded them all that he had little food but many instruments.

Harry lifted Carolyn off her chair, grabbed her hand, and led her out of the apartment. As they walked toward Washington Square Park, he put his hand around her shoulder and Carolyn melted into him. His thoughts and emotions were all over the place: He couldn't resist her, told himself to be away from her, was certain he would marry her. Neither of them said a word until Harry suggested, "If we don't get nailed by a flying Frisbee, maybe we can try singing together there. I stuck the lyrics in my back pocket."

They were each twenty-two, birthdays months apart, and Carolyn wondered whether they were too young to marry. She thought about it as she reached around his jeans, gently touching him, and withdrew the paper with the words on it. Logically, she needed space, as she had just begun to create in Boston, to think about who she was and what she wanted. Yes, he was hypnotically attractive to her, but her friends warned her about the dangers of having a one and only and how it might not last. Her snapshot of the current moment, though, made her hopeful. Besides, they had just moved into the apartment. She wanted to give it a chance. He had this offbeat charm, a self-effacing boyish enthusiasm. He made her jump. She wanted to tumble, with him, down a sand dune, climb back up, and roll all the way to the seashore somewhere. Carolyn visualized that scene as they made their way to the park. Harry took out a few crumpled notes when they got there. Every time he sat down, Harry crushed whatever he had in that back pocket.

They leaned against the back of a park bench, and Harry began to softly sing from "People Will Say We're in Love."

Carolyn couldn't help herself. "We are," she said.

"Okay," said Harry. "It really isn't so terrible to fall for someone." He hesitated before adding, "I guess that's obvious."

"I'm just a little over the moon, too," Carolyn said and pushed his hair aside to kiss him. They embraced and pressed together, unabashedly passionate in the middle of the city park.

"I just hope I can be good enough," said Harry. "I went through a folk phase when we were apart. I kept thinking of that Tom Paxton line—you know, the one about loving you better. I just don't want to disappoint you." Carolyn shook her head and hugged him even harder. Harry said, "Listen, we said we would get to Edison's by 2:00."

Carolyn looked up and saw what she imagined was a white dove above her, even though she knew that doves could not possibly be twenty feet off the ground in Washington Square Park. It was probably just a local pigeon taking a tour; she knew that doves were mostly Texas residents. She was aware that Harry was talking about Edison and wondering whether he might know a justice of the peace. Her own life was moving with such speed she could barely process things. What she did know was that they needed work—and that she was trusting a few people she met too recently. Harry was driven—to find friends, to marry her... She told him she saw a dove, and he gazed upward and said it was white but he wasn't a birder.

Off they went, zigzagging through walkers, joggers, parents wheeling strollers, and pavement musicians, jugglers, and portrait painters. They stopped for a moment to get frozen lemonades and pretzels, which would have to substitute for lunch. Harry began whistling, "People Will Say We're in Love." Carolyn jabbed him in the ribs and questioned how he had learned how to whistle. Harry quickly replied that his dad was a whistling master and that it was inevitable that he would inherit the knack. The two of them then raced off laughing and arrived at 24 Houston out of breath yet happy. Neither had thought to bring the key to the outside door, so they hit the button by Edison's name on the directory and he buzzed them through.

He greeted them with, "I get the first love thing and I can imagine more than that, but you got to remember your keys, kids. True, one of us is usually here, but unless you're the president of the country or mayor of New York City, you need your own keys. You want drinks? You both look winded. Coke? They nodded, and Edison was soon back with two Cokes and an unopened box of assorted donuts. He picked out the first two, explaining that he could never decide between chocolate and glazed. "I also see everything through music."

"I catch that for sure," said Harry. "Where are you going with this?"

"I live with music but no other humans. I do have a special place for kids," Edison answered.

"So, you see that we kind of like each other and we're both into music and you're putting this together," Carolyn said.

With that, Edison went to the piano and explained that finding a song that worked for both of them was the priority. Harry suggested something with "Honey dear, won't you be mine?" in it, while Carolyn sang and Edison created a melody.

"Is this vintage Elvis or early Beatles?" Harry asked.

Before anyone could answer, Rosie appeared and carried with her plastic cups, and Lola, holding a large bottle of red wine to her chest. Beaming, they came into Edison's living room. Carolyn thought they could pass for sisters and wondered, out loud, whether they could complete each other's sentences.

"Would that mean that I can qualify as a brother?" Edison asked. "I didn't have any sisters—at least until now."

With that, Rosie and Lola joked about fattening up Edison further while admitting that he wasn't quite the skinny thing he was when they first met him.

Rosie asked him whether the kids had come through, and he told them about the song they were writing.

Lola said, "I think we need to take a vote before this cool guy actually becomes our brother. I have to seriously consider. Our tight-knit, little community might not be enough. I suggest we draw blood and mix it together. Then again, Richard might not like that idea so much. What do you think, Rosie? Your kids will probably hear about it, too."

Rosie assured everyone that Richard really did like the group but was just on such a crazy work schedule that he was usually sleeping when the rest of the world was awake. "I don't know how long we deal with his shifts and, in a sense, being apart," she said before adding, "I would rather get back to this next generation right here."

"Guess that's me," said Carolyn. "The way you three look out for each other is what the two of us want. I mean, yeah, high expectations for us." She laced her fingers together. "When I was growing up, a little boy in our neighborhood taught me the church, steeple, people hand game. He and Harry have whistling in common. The little kid, though, could do that with a blade of grass. He had pet turtles."

At this point, Edison cut in. "Like I was saying," he said, "we try to find an original and bring it to an open mic, try it out. So far, it's 'We live, we love, add one and the other, two of us forever, oh yeah, hitched together.' Hokey, maybe, but if we can arrange voices on this and add another lyric line or two, we got something." Edison shrugged his shoulders.

***

Four months later, with Thanksgiving fast approaching, Carolyn was still uncertain. They had wowed a small audience on open mic night at a nearby club, and Edison was pushing for much more. Harry would refer to a house frame as a symbol and claimed they had already filled it in, at least partially. Carolyn was nervous about spending the upcoming holiday with Harry's parents. More urgently, she was not ready for the home that would first feature a dog and then a child. Harry forced himself to focus on a dog, hoping the responsibility would become a stepping-stone. Carolyn needed to be herself, and the current coupling with Harry was plenty for the moment.

In retrospect, Harry was grateful for his time as a census worker, glad that he had stayed in long enough to at least have an identity. He initially kept a log and tally sheet as he knocked on doors. His explanatory notes sometimes spoke of percentages. He wrote, for example, that "Almost all of the old-world Jews whom I've tried to befriend are wary of me, and some are just terrified. Of me? Maybe they think I have a knife in a side pocket of my shorts or they don't like my hair, stubble beard, old T-shirts. One guy actually yelled at me to stay, then smelled my breath and scolded me not to drink anymore. I'm not much of an alcohol guy. The problem is that I could not keep my distance all the time and still get information. If they left the door open a crack or even talked through the chain, it was possible to score something or other.

"The most welcoming people were immigrants from Puerto Rico, who were naturally, often-times without hesitation, open to conversation. They were more than thrilled to be wedged into an overcrowded Lower East Side apartment. Kids flocked to me when I came through the door, and one family even invited me to dinner. The folks next door asked me in for dessert.

"Drugged-out hippies were a mixed bag since smoke was all over the place but pretty much everyone was okay about sharing stuff. Most asked me to come in, and one couple actually pulled me right in. They thought I looked like them. I never did indulge in much more than weed because I was scared of mescaline and LSD. No, I was never an acid head."

As time went on, he became more determined to win over the hearts of at least one or two resettled Jews who looked to be ancient. They were fixtures, never budging from Houston Street. Harry even put on khaki shorts, instead of usual denim cutoffs, and chose a button-down short-sleeved shirt. He even tied his hair back.

Receiving no answer to one set of short raps on an apartment door, he leaned into the small, circular window that allowed patrons and visitors alike to eye one another.

"What do you want, young man?" asked the person on the other side of the glass.

"1970 census," said Harry, staying on script.

Typically, this would shut off a conversation. This time, though, a man wearing a yarmulke slowly opened a creaky door. "I don't know about census, but you, young man, are persistent. Come in."

Having broken through at last, Harry was uncertain as he tentatively stepped into an entry room. An aroma of meat, probably pot roast, permeated the air. This, to Harry, was familiar and comforting.

The man grasped Harry's elbow and led him to the kitchen, where he pulled forward two chairs. "Sit. I am Abram. Feel free to call me Abe," said the man, who simultaneously smiled and looked directly into Harry's eyes.

"Harry. Just Harry."

"What, you must attach a word to describe your name? My next questions are connected: Why census? What's so valuable about a stack of numbers?"

"That's what I thought. I took the job because my best friend and I planned to do this together. Then he died—just like that. Gone. I have that as a reason, and now I need money. I actually like the part about meeting people. I never imagined I would. I expected I would ring a bell, drop off the form if no one was there, or get the information. Case closed, move on. My first few hours on the job, I fell way, way behind. I guess this is telling me something about who I am and what I want to do."

"Young man, do not make a career of census taking. It won't add up to a hill of beans, and you will get bored. Believe me," said Abram.

"Why are you different from the rest?" Harry asked. "Who lives here?" He looked around and saw that Abram's walls were filled with photographs. Each picture was perfectly positioned next to another; nothing was haphazard. One could appreciate the specificity from afar and admire the artwork up close. Harry saw one label: "Personal Family." The group included two sets of photos in vertical configuration.

"Did you take any of them?" asked Harry.

"My eye is better used for framing and providing perspective. The answer to your question is yes. If I have any skill, it is to support talent," said Abram. He then prodded Harry to pull up a chair and inspect the photographs unhurriedly and closely. Abram told Harry to cover one eye first and then the other as he placed his head at various angles. Abram continued, "Look at more than one at a time. Stand up and look down on them. Experiment." All of which indicated that Abram felt an observer, an audience member, would be better served by that person's unique imagination.

Hence, Harry proceeded by squinting and then opening his eyes wide. When Harry placed his face inches from one image, he saw that the young woman and Abram shared the same nose, long yet ramrod straight. "This is your sister?" he asked.

"Good. You've relaxed enough to concentrate, and that is the pivotal component: easing your mind to then intensely take in what is before you. Those who catapult quickly forward cannot possibly appreciate so keenly," he said.

"Religion or art—which is more important? I mean, to you?" asked Harry.

"I've had this kippah on my head for much of my life. When I shed it, I feel undressed," said Abram. "That's all." When Harry pressed for more explanation, Abram said, "Under Jewish law, you wear it. I accepted this—I don't know why—without challenging, and I've been wearing this skull piece forever. I put on my underwear; I put on my yarmulke. Okay?"

Harry was not sure he did understand, but he switched the subject to his friendship with the three people he knew living at 24 Houston. He asked Abram if he had ever met Edison.

"We've seen one another at the outdoor market—pear aficionados we are. Also, part of an artists' collective," said Abram.

Harry leaned forward and said, "Ed wants us to sing with him, at clubs maybe. And no, I wouldn't call him anything but Edison to his face."

"So, who is 'us'?" asked Abram.

"Me and my girlfriend, Carolyn, who could be a rockstar. That's what I think. I guess I'm just musical enough and make my voice passable to sing with her," added Harry.

"Modesty becomes you, young man," Abram said. He waited a moment before adding, "You're gentle."

They continued the back-and-forth as Abram explained that he lived by himself but was friendly with Rosie and Lola. Abram was actually a bit jealous that Harry lived within a floor of them. Harry said he and Carolyn felt almost like they had been adopted by the women and Edison.

"This country more or less adopted my family," said Abram. "My ancestors came across the ocean to Ellis Island. Listen, you are sweet and also honest. I know nothing of your girlfriend, but I will assume the same of her. My free advice to you is to go off, see a part of this country together. The trip will tell you more than setting up here in the city. Go."

Before he did, however, Harry once again asked Abram for census details. His lips lifting toward a grin, Abram filled out the form, pointed on the page to his phone number, and requested that Harry call him. Processing all that he could, Harry eagerly set out for home while considering Abram's recommendation that he and Carolyn explore another part of the country. Aside from Boston forays, neither had strayed far from what everyone called metropolitan New York. Harry was wary of the clichéd "go with what you know." He knew that seeking and stretching would fuel his relationship with Carolyn. Dashing along the sidewalk now, he convinced himself that she would agree. How could she not? But where should they go? He didn't know anything about the rest of the country. When he had left early that morning, Carolyn had told him she was working on music they could sing together. When Harry burst through the apartment door, he found Carolyn sitting at the old, lopsided wooden table in their kitchen, a hand-me-down from her parents. She was seriously considering whether this thing with Harry was just too rushed and risky, even though she knew she loved him.

Brief Moab Memory

Harry and Carolyn, mutually lustful that summer of 1970, left the big city a couple of weeks before Labor Day and flew to Moab, Utah. Harry's research turned up a popular place twenty-something miles south called Hole 'N' the Rock. He convinced Carolyn that he would propose if they found their way to that spot. He discovered this cave was a favorite gathering place for cowboys back in the

1940s. Since he and Carolyn had both grown up watching westerns on TV, they were intrigued.

Finally arriving after multiple plane flights, Carolyn realized it was just too much to think about Hole 'N' the Rock. After all, they sought obscurity and romance rather than tourist-trap scenarios. On the main drag through town, gas stations, and motels, along with many an aging car, beckoned Harry and Carolyn. One sign encouraged manufacturing. Harry felt guilty, and Carolyn wondered whether she should have resisted this trip.

They settled on the Utes Motel for accommodations. It wasn't much in terms of amenities, but it did offer privacy. Harry signed them in as Harry and Carolyn Edison. It was an homage to Edison, back on Houston Street, who had echoed Abram's suggestion to get out of town. "You're hot for each other—get out!" he had implored. But Moab?

The air conditioner in their room on the strip in Moab worked only on "fan," so it blew in heat. The temperature outside was mid-nineties and dry. They, though, were sweaty young lovers, so who cared? The Utes Motel, funky yet functional, fit their needs.

They ventured outside to the nearby diner for lunch and every other day for breakfast, too. The motel carried small boxes of cereal, which they munched without milk. Dinner was pizza or hamburgers, all served at the same place.

Harry and Carolyn didn't care to drive somewhere to hike. The cross street led upward, and walks there were richly fulfilling. They had to be out during early morning or after sunset to avoid the scorching heat.

Years later, when they'd accumulated inheritance dollars just sufficient to allow Harry and Carolyn to have a house of moderate build in Moab, their memories of the small motel remained delectably alive.

Now, the lovers found a justice of the peace, exchanged personal vows each had written down, and placed rings on each other's fingers. For better or worse, they would return to New York as a married couple. Their parents did not know, but their new friends figured it out.

NYC

Ten hours later, they were sitting in Rosie's apartment with Edison, Lola, Rosie, and Richard. Rosie shooed her kids away with the "big people's talk, get out" explanation.

Even Edison, who had urged them to "just do it," was surprised Harry and Carolyn had followed through. "You mean you just searched the Yellow Pages for a J.P. and that was it?" he asked.

"We took the advice of the guy who ran the motel," said Harry.

"He just pointed at a two-story building. We went there, found a nice man who was more than willing to help us, and here we are."

"What was this Moab like? I've never heard of it," said Lola.

"We planned to do some hiking, but we spent a lot of time in our room," said Carolyn.

"With protection, I hope," said Rosie.

Even while exhausted, Carolyn reddened while nodding her head.

"Sharp rings," said Richard, causing Harry to laugh. He didn't know if Richard was being honest or playfully joking. Carolyn and Harry had only seen Richard one time previously.

Part II

Chapter 3

Moab

May 2010

BOYS AND GIRLS MET at Delicate Arch where, having taxed their growing bodies for more than an hour hiking up smooth rocks and boulders, they were able to sit, joke, and ponder. It was some time since anyone slipped backward and skidded down the gully toward the ravine below.

These adolescents grew familiar with themselves and the formations. That the arch was copper in color does not faze them. Growing up here afforded an understanding: The rock formations struck the eyes as golden, red, rust, and even silver according to either atmospheric conditions or one's personal perception.

Diana liked to sweat because she thought it was sexy. She reached the final plateau, turned around, and raced back down or around the periphery until her hairline was wet. Her tank top adhered to her chest, and this very much pleased her since she was certain the look attractive men. She was certain she read that somewhere.

Her boyfriend, LG, sat and stared at tourists who, exhausted, contemplated whether or not to continue a hike along the river. *Moment of truth*, he thought. He noticed that a new fold of flesh gathered about his waist. Always skinny, he now drank beer often. He wondered whether he would soon brag about a fully rounded potbelly—like his father's. Of course, he hadn't seen the man in years. LG was curious about the future but was not worried. Diana would still like him; if she grew tired, he would look elsewhere. Besides, girls ween't his primary interest.

Diana, on the other hand, squeezed the skin around her nearly taut middle, fretful that she would develop what she'd read were a girl's love handle. Barely a hundred pounds, she was terrified to the point that she ate infrequently. As she walked around the final turn before the landing came into view, she imagined LG's hand encircling her hips. She turned toward the canyon side and smiled to herself.

Tomorrow, Marissa, Diana's big sister, and Carrie, Marissa's best friend from high school, would arrive. Marissa, seven years older than Diana, sometimes called New Jersey home, even while currently living in Brooklyn. Diana, though, was attached to Moab, where she now resided for a few years.

Marissa and Carrie had last spent time together at their high school's fifth reunion for the class of 1999. Carrie had handed Marissa a copy of "Tell Me," a short story Carrie read in an independent Berkeley journal she and several other grad students had independently published.

Marissa was an actress and Carrie a playwright. The plan they formulated was that Carrie would write Marissa into her plays. Carrie told Marissa that when they met at Delicate Arch, she would reveal Marissa's role in the play. But a few days ago, Carrie had called with bad news.

"I have mononucleosis," she had said. "They won't let me out of this room. I'm sorry."

Marissa had been counting down the days in anticipation of the rendezvous.

"That's okay. I'll be seeing my sister anyway," she said, failing to camouflage her disappointment. "Aren't you a bit long in the tooth to be coming down with mono?"

In truth, Marissa wished she could simply cancel the trip. She was East Coast, and Moab was nowhere. It wasn't that she wanted to neglect her little sister, but she had a play coming up in Alphabet City and she would rather stay in Brooklyn, walk over the bridge, and rehearse. She realized that Diana missed her, but where and how could their worlds possibly intersect? There were some pretty cool places in Moab, but Diana was often solitary, choosing to stay by herself even when she had other, creative options.

Marissa, at this point, hated total silence. Last time she was in Moab, she found herself awakened by a lonely rooster's morning call. Nobody else stirred. Marissa realized she now had a lot of city in her. Still, she would get on that plane to Salt Lake City. Might as well go through with it.

⚘⚘⚘⚘⚘ ⚘⚘⚘⚘⚘

Her flight arrived early, and Marissa settled into the rented Sebring convertible and the high-speed ride to Moab. She was not more than thirty miles away before she realized she had forgotten to tell Diana that Carrie had canceled. Marissa grabbed her cell phone but stopped short of calling Diana. Might as well go through the story just once rather than on the phone and then again in person.

Marissa and Diana had always been physical opposites. Marissa's breasts and hips expanded early on. Her natural curves snapped men's heads but displeased her. Never could she find a bra that truly fit. She wore a large men's hoodie when she jogged to cover up and camouflage her body.

Diana, pencil thin, never trusted a scale, always claimed she needed to lose a pound, and frequently found her way to a bathroom after eating. Other women shook their heads and looked away when Diana complained about her weight. She claimed the bathroom scale was her enemy.

Neither especially condoned nor respected the other's self-perception.

Diana obsessed about her silhouette and longed to wear a fuller cup.

Marissa wished she could jump, hike, swim, or bike without bouncing around. No wonder she always passed on playing mixed-doubles tennis.

From the neck up, however, their features were strikingly similar: high foreheads; bushy, dark brows; small, straight noses; one dimple each on either side of the full lips; and bright, strong teeth.

Convinced it would enhance her love life, Diana had dyed her hair golden red when she was seventeen and never looked back. Marissa kept hers at shoulder length and highlighted the chestnut with gold.

Each was a catch—for different types of men.

Marissa wished she could stay to herself, or home, or out of men's focus. This never worked. Shortly after her fourteenth birthday, older boys began calling her, grabbing at her, pursuing her, or, specifically, groping her chest. The first male who looked her straight in the eye, she half-seriously remarked, she would marry. Meanwhile, her parents, Harry and Carolyn, insisted that she bury herself in schoolbooks. "Boyfriends are nothing but a pain in the behind," said her father.

Boys hit on Diana. She kept them at arm's length as if she could literally push at their foreheads and remain virtuous.

Marissa often wished she were the little sister. Now, as ever, she would have to present herself as the adult, the mature young woman on the up but never on the make. What a curse, what a crock!

She drove up to Eklectica, the designated restaurant that Marissa realized Diana had selected in an attempt to please her, and jerked the rental to a halt.

Climbing out of the driver-side door, she said, "Power breaks; I'm not used to that," and then thought, *What a dumb, inappropriate greeting.*

Diana rushed up but mimed a hug, barely grazing her sister's shoulders.

Each wanted what the other had.

"No matter how often I've come, it's always amazing here," said Marissa. "Opposite of metro New York."

"Yeah, I live here now. No humidity," said Diana.

"But hot in the summer, yes?"

"The good part is that I don't eat much for three months," said Diana.

"Dee, really, you haven't gained an ounce."

Diana cut her off. "Look," she said, grasping for a smidgeon of spare flesh.

Marissa began to laugh, then checked herself. "Diana, I'm glad to see you."

"Me, too," said Diana.

The sisters hugged, as if to begin anew.

"Lunch then?" asked Marissa.

"Sure."

They sat outside, finding a set-up for children that had tiny, red vinyl chairs and a tiny table to match.

"I forgot how beautiful it is out here," said Marissa. "It's earth colors—the reds, browns, corals... I sort of remember that. Totally blanked on the river."

"It's kind of isolating here. I mean, look around, Issa."

"That's what I've been doing on the drive, Dee. It's nothing like the Northeast. Not that much green, except the Colorado River. Back home, you get everything lush: trees, plants, the lawns obsessive homeowners cultivate. And you can drive to the Berkshires and Vermont for incredible woods. Nothing, though, matches the vistas, the space, here. I already feel released."

"That's funny because I feel like a prisoner."

"So why do you stay?"

"LG, for one thing. Plus, I have a job and know my way around. That's not saying a whole lot about either my boyfriend or working in the bookstore."

Neither chose, during those initial moments, to mention their parents.

Marissa realized they had placed their order long ago. "Does the waitress appear often or only between breaks?" she asked.

"You sound so New York—which isn't all that uncommon out here," said Diana, "or necessarily off base. The pace is slower here, much slower, often too slow to suit me. Then again, climbing a tough rock is a big deal."

"Now you sound like the sarcastic snob from back East," said Marissa.

"What happened to Carrie—is it okay to ask?

"Mono. She had to cancel."

"People your age can get mono? I never knew that," said Diana. "Unless she's fooling around with teenage boys."

Marissa tried to smother her laughter, but then she let loose and the two young women began to howl.

"My boyfriend had mono. Then again, he will kiss any girl, even anything female," said Diana, setting off the sisters once again. "How's your love life, sis?"

"I move from one neurotic New York man to the next. The only things that change are hairlines and waistlines. It's like hook up and move on. You've been together with this PG for some time now, haven't you?"

"It's LG, and it's been more than half a year, which, for me, is like a lifetime," said Diana. "I'm supposed to meet him for a walk later. Wanna come?"

"I haven't even dropped my stuff off yet or, for that matter, eaten anything. I mean, do they have to catch the food out here or import all of it?

Assuming we get served, yeah, after you show me my room or my bed or my futon or my mattress or my spot on the floor, I'm up for exploring. Gotta be safer than the subway."

At that moment, a waiter returned. Bald on top, the remaining hair ponytailed, he smiled sweetly, then said, "We're out of salmon, but we took the liberty of doing trout for you. It's actually more expensive, and when we have had to substitute it in the past, no one ever complains. On the contrary, people thank us."

"That explains you, Marissa," Diana said. "But what about my burger?"

"We're actually doing it over. Let's just put it this way: We were distracted. It was a conversation about the Colorado and keeping it clean. Someone said we shouldn't allow them to shoot mega-movies out here. You know. So instead of giving you a dish that tastes like shoe leather, we're cooking it as we speak—and keeping an eye on it this time."

Within ten minutes, both orders appeared. The young women abandoned their conversation to focus on the food—and heartily consumed it.

The waiter, incongruously named Bugsy, sat one table away, turned his attention and his face to the sun, and baked contentedly. Every so often, he swiveled toward Marissa and Diana and, without speaking, established eye contact to make certain all was well.

When they were finished, the sisters, without risking further delay by asking for a check, computed the tip, tipped generously, and walked swiftly to Marissa's rental. Bugsy, by now, had fallen asleep as his entire head reddened.

Marissa was used to the green lawns, bushes, shrubs, and trees of the Northeast. Here, the slick rock, canyons of sandstone, vistas of deep pink mixed with beige, and the ever-widening sky seemed to hold a brilliant surprise as her eye scanned the horizon. She felt insignificant in comparison to the "set." *That is*, she thought, *what it is: the set for an ongoing outdoor production.*

And wasn't that what this area was about? Thrill seekers taking the fourteen-mile bicycle ride atop the boulders? Jeepsters and Hummer drivers angling the vehicles at seventy-five percent or more, risking self-spillage and not-so-secretly hoping for a tumble so that they could then live to embellish the tale? Rafters wishing for a current that might dump them into the icy Colorado, which stretched through seven states and Mexico, too?

Marissa was a soft, curvy girl of the suburbs. If she were more sinewy, would she then wish to challenge, dare, thrust herself against the elements in such a land as this? Diana

had been living in the house their parents had built years before. Harry and Carolyn had chosen to keep the structure and encouraged Diana to live there with minimal expense. She had transformed the interior, leaving only her parents' bedroom as it was.

Marissa was delighted and impressed to find that Diana had updated the inside. In addition to painting the walls in various rooms apricot, deep royal blue, burgundy, and yellow, she had changed the color in the living area from tan to off-white and mounted art posters—some found, some purchased—on the walls.

Marissa collapsed atop and then within a collection of extra-large pillows that backed up into a triangular V in one corner of the sprawling room.

"This place has warmth, feels like home," she said.

"For now," said Diana. "LG and I were thinking of moving in together. But that was when he seemed to care about something—anything."

"What does he do?"

"He works at a store, then he smokes weed after work. Every so often, he shows up here."

"Why do you stay with him?"

"Go on that walk with me. You'll see."

Marissa was not aware that she had fallen asleep. It seemed hours but was actually fifteen minutes later that Diana stood over her, gently urging her to wake up. They would soon need to leave to make it to Arches on time to meet up with LG.

Marissa did not care about going but remembered that she had agreed to do so. With animation, she shook her head, steadied herself, and wandered toward the hallway and, she hoped, a bathroom. When she looked in the mirror, Marissa saw that her naturally raven, thick hair, when she fully combed it out, nearly reached her deepening cleavage. No wonder men rarely looked her in the eye. She splashed water on her face, stared at herself, and tried to accept the woman she saw.

LG

Larry Gold went by LG Appleton because he liked the name and didn't wish to risk revealing his Jewish identity. Even out here, someone might figure that Gold had been shortened from Goldblum or Goldenberg. With his sandy hair and expanding gut, he looked the part of a townie. He liked to smoke, drink, fool around on the guitar, and write poetry. Women fell for his green eyes, and some even seemed to enjoy his girth. Well, Diana would have preferred him skinny. No matter. He would continue to whisper to himself, "Thin might be in, but fat's where it's at."

He had plenty of time before he was to meet her, so he stretched out and lounged by the Colorado. He took out a reporter's notebook, which fit snugly into the back pocket of his jeans, and thought about writing. He had been thinking about the name Moab. Why Moab?

He had taken the time at the café in Eddie McStiff's to research the word and was still a bit confused at what he'd found. Maybe that was because the only source he located was the Catholic Encyclopedia. LG was hoping to make a connection between Biblical Moab and the place where he lived. Yes, it was more than 4,000 feet above sea level back in the day. He knew that was the elevation in town. The mountains must be twice as high, and La Sal—well, everyone knew that range was 10,000 feet up. He once was up there with a girl named Crystal, but that was long before Diana had come into the picture.

Now, he stared out at the horizon and thought about John Wayne. The old Apache Motel was named for the dude. As he dozed in the sun, LG thought maybe he could become the new John Wayne. He was already big enough, and he'd been with more than a couple of women. Wayne must have spent some time at bars—or saloons, as they were called in the movies LG had seen.

He wasn't all that motivated to do much of anything and moved from job to job. Now, he was working at a convenience store and training to lead Hummer tours. Now that, LG liked: scaring a bunch of fat cat tourists by jacking up the ATV like it might really tip over. Also, you could get by on some of the tips people, especially guys from back East, would leave.

He fell asleep and probably would have missed making the date with Diana if a bad-ass car with a bum muffler hadn't jarred him awake. He ambled over to his car, realizing he needed to speed to the parking area, then book it up the slick rocks to even have a shot at being fashionably late. Back when he was in shape, maybe that would have been possible. Now, what with smoking cigarettes and joints, and the belly, he wasn't certain. On the other hand, he was still muscular, except his midsection. Maybe, for a change, he would keep his shirt on. After all, he didn't really have any abs to show. Every so often, he thought about doing a sit-up. Or quitting the sauce.

❧ ☙

Diana appreciated having a big sister. It became so much easier for Dee because Marissa paved the way. Serving as a buffer to their parents, Marissa was bold and determined in her defense of Diana each time the kid sibling strayed off the liberal foot-path.

Marissa enjoyed taking care of her cute little sister. Diana, for the longest time, had looked up to, checked in with, felt protected by, and generally idolized Marissa. The past several years had been necessary for separation. Diana needed to get away from the East, and she had done well just to survive out here. But Marissa was worried about the boyfriend since Diana made it sound like she was both besotted with him and cynical about the relationship.

Finally, it was about time to meet the mysterious LG and make her own judgment.

Diana drove out of the neighborhood, and within moments, they were beyond the Visitors Center and on the road to Delicate Arch. They had left plenty of time, and Marissa knew she was gawking at the rock formations. So many, she felt, had signature faces. Some frowned, while others cast coy glances at all the sluggish tourists. Marissa squinted, hoping to disguise herself, as if the Balanced Rock might turn on her and ask what a girl from the New York City suburbs was doing out this way.

"Marissa, look at the arch over there," said Diana as she pointed. "It's Skyline."

Marissa, used to Brooklyn and the New York cityscape, had forgotten about Moab's stark beauty. She opened her mouth but stared silently.

LG took each curve at sixty miles per hour, no matter the advisory. He had been driving since he was fifteen and, despite a few accidents, showed no fear when behind the wheel. Bikes thrilled him, and a hot, twisting car ride through the canyon was the next best thing.

Diana saw him careening behind her as she neared the parking area. She edged her car into a place as LG came to a screeching halt in the next space over.

"You got me, Dee," he said.

She wasn't certain of the context. "Whichever way you mean it, LG, you'll get no argument from me. This is Issa." Realizing her intro sounded like someone practicing a consonant drill, Diana rephrased. "My sister, Marissa," she said, without whistling her s's.

"So this is your famous boyfriend," said Marissa. "She has great things to say about you." Marissa looked him up and down, thinking to herself that he must be wild in bed.

LG sucked in while simultaneously tugging his T-shirt downward. He returned Marissa's gaze, noting the family resemblance—except for Marissa's upper body. LG looked at her directly and then forced himself to turn toward Diana. Regrouping, he smiled.

"I fell asleep by the river. Had to rocket myself over here to make it on time. We set for the climb to Delicate, Dee?"

"That was the idea, LG."

"What's that mean?"

"Just that you and I had discussed this. Marissa's never been."

"Right."

The trail walk was deceptive. No one would imagine the smooth rocks, the incline, the length of the hike ahead. Impossible? No. But it did require some degree of fitness and was not quite a stroll in the park.

Diana took pride in her conditioning and modified her parents' home just a bit At home, mirrors lined the walls as she exercised, allowing her to watch carefully as her body gyrated to her workout CD. She never liked what she saw but knew enough to struggle against eating disorder. Still, those who knew her wished she would pack on at least five or even ten more pounds. Her flesh stretched to cover her bones.

Just now, she was scooting along. Why hesitate?

Marissa kept her little sister and LG within sight if not shouting distance. Far from overweight, she was wasp-waisted. Men were entranced with her figure. She knew that women were jealous as well.

Marissa caught herself eyeing the couple yards ahead of her. That relationship, she thought, will never last if the kid gains any more weight. Dee was such a nut about calories. From the rear, this boy, LG, looked pretty cool. The front, though, was a different story. These days, thought Marissa, Diana probably had more than a handful of him.

Marissa's last beau, William, was also in the midst of a horizontal growth spurt. She didn't mind. He was cute—like a big teddy bear, soft and cuddly. Who really cared what he would look like at forty? Better to be with a man who appreciated her. She had had her share of bad boyfriends. William was okay for a time but not forever.

LG pulled up to catch his breath, and within moments, Marissa approached the pair. She reached for Diana's shoulder to steady herself.

"This is where the hike actually begins," said LG. "They ought to post a sign. It's not exactly a beginner's walk. It's worth it, though, especially if you're not afraid of heights. Delicate Arch is the coolest."

"Scary, too," said Diana.

"Like you, Dee," he replied.

LG struck a pose out of the 1950s he had rehearsed many times before. He lacked only a pack of cigarettes jammed beneath the shoulder portion of a plain white T-shirt. Instead, he carried his smokes in his back pocket, hoping Diana would not notice. He thought of the physical resemblance between the sisters. If only Diana would let herself go a little bit. He wouldn't mind having something to grab onto.

Each time they showered together, there was so much less of her. Maybe to balance him. And she was starting to comment about his paunch. He did not find her remarks all that amusing. This, he was positive, was the start of trouble.

She touched him on the nape of the neck, one of his favorite spots, and LG's world, for that instant, was perfect. How could he ever, ever think anything bad about her? He wished he could take her in his arms right now, hide away beneath the arch, and make frantic love until the sun went down.

Marissa again reached for Diana's shoulder but caught, instead, her sister's elbow, causing the women to tumble sideways. Luckily, they fell to red clay, rolling over on top of each other. LG covered his mouth, lest he laugh too hard.

As they rose, each one dusted the dirt out of the other's hair. Diana scowled until she saw that Marissa's T-shirt had ridden up, allowing for a rock to wedge in her waistband. LG plucked the stone, held it up to the sun, and pretended to assess it.

"Maybe we should call it a day," he said. "You two are still smiling after having done your synchronized fall here. Let's not push it. What do you say? We could go to the Broken Oar for a drink."

"Oh, that's all you need," said Diana.

"Sis, it's okay. He looks good, by the way. I don't need to see Delicate. I once hiked all the way."

"Once. We're more than halfway there. Why not just get up and around? It's a little bit more exciting than settling for a beer and a burger."

LG and Marissa had already turned around. Diana was outnumbered and not in the mood to fight both her boyfriend and her sister. The walk back down was trickier than the walk up had been. Diana was wary: Smooth rocks occasionally precipitated turned ankles. Despite her premonition, that journey was uneventful.

⁂

Marissa had never been to the Broken Oar, but she felt comfortable immediately. Used to a very different dating scene in the Jersey 'burbs and boroughs of Manhattan and Brooklyn, she was relieved to watch men and women operating more directly.

Her imagined conversation: "Want sex?"

"Sure."

"Where?"

"Your place?"

"When?"

"The sooner, the better."

Marissa envisioned someone hitting on her.

She did not expect, just then, a prep-alum suitor, complete with his collar pushed up against the back of his neck, to approach her. He looked like he had stepped off the pages of an Abercrombie & Fitch ad.

"Not many people around here look like you," he said, with the touch of a well-worn sledgehammer.

She turned away toward Diana and, she hoped, LG. He was perched upon a bar stool, happily stirring a mixed drink.

The stranger continued, "Could I buy you something like that?"

She thought that was pretty lame. Couldn't he offer a martini or something?

Trained to be ever polite, she said, "That would be nice. Gin and bitter lemon, thank you."

He tossed a command over his shoulder. "G with bitter," he said. She could not recall such an abbreviation.

"I'm not one to go after women. Check it out, though," he said, gesturing toward the other patrons. "Not one woman with class, serenity. You are a breath of the Northeast, shall I say?"

"You're right on the geography. But I'm not the picture of serenity—inside or out," said Marissa.

"Ah, the actor within. That explains your demeanor, no?"

"I suppose so. While I hesitate to actually call myself a theater person, that description comes closer than any high and mighty intellectual explanation," she noted. "I did some acting in high school, yes. Still trying."

Diana and LG snuggled up to the counter on bar stools, matching shots with laughter as they pawed at one another.

"That's my sister," said Marissa. "I don't even know your name."

"Grant," he said.

"Grant? As in Cary?"

"I was raised in Larchmont, and my parents met at Ethical Culture in Manhattan." He paused. "That says plenty to you, doesn't it?"

"I understand," said Marissa.

"Let me show you around?" asked Grant.

"I've been here before—I mean, to Moab—but why not? Just don't take advantage," she joked, at least partially hopeful that he would sweep her off her feet.

Diana turned her head just in time to see Marissa mouth, "I'm out of here," while pointing toward Grant. Diana understood that her sister had plans.

Diana smiled and gave Marissa a thumbs-up. She caught up with LG, who touched her shoulder and then placed a hand across her buttocks. The move wasn't terribly subtle—not that she minded. She felt the heat and swayed backward into him.

"Marissa, LG's been after me to help him buy some pants. He's, you know, getting a little bigger. He needs more room."

Marissa realized both the truth as well as the code. She recognized that look. This time, it was she who gave the thumbs-up. Marissa hooked her hand around Grant's waist. He, in turn, extended his long arm and palm fully beyond hers.

What in this world was she doing with a man she had known for ten minutes? Maybe this really was the Wild Wild West—the land of good guys, bad guys, easy women, and impossibly far-fetched love stories. *Still to be determined*, she thought.

While her big sister wondered whether Diana and LG would survive,

Diana realized her attraction to him had been primarily physical and perhaps she had been convincing herself that he was Mr. Right. That was twenty pounds ago.

He was bringing her to a convenience store before going back, he said, to his place.

"What now, L?"

"Maybe a Drake's," he said.

Diana sighed, laughed, and forced herself to avoid making a sarcastic crack.

"What is this, Diana? Every second, you're on my case about a couple of extra pounds."

"It impacts my life—our sex life, or what's left of it," she said.

"At least I'm not skin and bones," he replied.

She was shocked. She ran, biked, hiked, and went to the gym on off days. Stared down even the hint of extra flesh in the full-length mirror. Now this? He wanted fat?

Diana turned her head toward the car window so that he wouldn't see the tear welling up in her eye. Instead of giving in, though, she gathered herself.

"I will gain three pounds if you lose five."

"Sounds like a deal for you," he said.

"I can't stand the thought of putting on five pounds. I'll look like a blimp."

"Dee, you need more weight on you—I mean, just to be healthy."

She took pride in running up hills hundreds of yards at a time. She never thought about the decision to wear nothing more than a tight-fitting jogging bra. It was comfortable, and she tried to convince herself it was okay — the way she looked when she checked the mirror.

"I like chocolate donuts," LG said. "They taste good. What can I say?"

"Exactly what you need."

"Look, if you want a six-pack stomach, maybe you should look elsewhere."

Shocked, she said, "I don't want anyone else. I'm just worried about you."

"That's nice, Diana. But it has more to do with my head than my midsection that I'm eating this way."

Again, she was startled. "What does that mean, LG?"

"It's not you and maybe even not me. Just here. I don't know if I want to be here. What do I do every day? Work, hang out, drink, eat, go to sleep. That's not a life, not the way I saw it a few years ago."

"What is it you're after, LG?"

"Truth is, I want to be married and start a family," he confessed.

She hadn't the slightest clue. Diana stared at him without saying a word.

"I know it doesn't look that way. But this is me."

Finally, Dee said, "You've never said even one word. In fact, I was pretty sure you weren't ready to stay with one woman. Lately, I've felt totally inadequate—like there was something I wasn't doing or saying. I don't know."

"It's not that I don't like you or love you. You're pretty fantastic. I've just been wondering if you wanted to have children. It's only around that, Diana."

"Yes," she said. "Definitely." But even as she blurted out the words, Diana was unsure of herself. "I've always envisioned having at least two kids, maybe more. What about careers, though? And what about me, when I look like a cow?"

"Forget the second part, Dee. The other one, yeah. Don't you get that I'm not the one who measures love by looks? That's you, and I'm guessing it must come from some deep, dark corner of your past. But Dee, frankly, I'm not into going there. Besides, you will only look like a dieting cow."

⁂

Marissa and Grant, meanwhile, moved along the Moab sidewalk. He said, "I'm not really the climb-every-mountain type. More like the sit-in-café caricature."

"I want to live in a city, like San Francisco," said Marissa. "Second choice: Boston. Not the suburbs. Tied for second: Brooklyn, where I am, not Manhattan. If they build up Brooklyn any further, make

Park Slope any more chi-chi, take it off the list. If the prices go up any further in San Francisco, take it off the list. That leaves Boston."

He smiled easily. "Which is probably too steep for either of our lists. Here I was wondering if my hamstrings would ever stand the hiking test."

"I'm not worried about your hamstrings, Grant."

With that, he kissed her on her hairline as she suspected he was aiming for her forehead.

They both laughed.

"So what are we doing in Moab of all places?" she asked. "Is that how things happen out here? You meet someone and the next thing you know, you're sharing life stories? I cannot believe you asked me if I wanted to see the sights of this town."

"I had to say something. I'm here because of the colors."

"Better keep going," she said.

"I'm doing research for a production set in the Southwest. I wanted to actually see the pinks, browns, beiges before we spread one inch of paint."

"And the people of Moab?" she asked.

"I had no idea," said Grant. "Bohemians who carry NRA cards loose in their back pockets?"

""I've visited Moab before, with my parents, at their house," said Marissa. Sort of know the territory by that.

Some are middle-aged or even older—former hippies—and others are cowboys. You have the Jeep guys, the rock climbers, the motor bikers, the tubers and rafters . . ."

". . . the people I saw last night who wouldn't qualify as poor people's Crosby, Stills, and Nash or The Dead . . . and us." Grant continued.

"Yes. . . us."

"So why do I find this at all appealing?" Grant asked. "It gets to something like 120 degrees in the shade in the summer."

"Maybe, just maybe, it's because there's a little less critiquing and judging out here. Do what you want, it seems to me, and people leave you alone," she said.

"Unlike New York."

"And I know we both love New York, but it sometimes does get to be a bit much," said Marissa.

"Maybe, then, we could take a weekend in a place like Santa Fe. Drive and sleep," said Grant.

"Find a health spa?" asked Marissa.

"With clothing optional," he added.

Marissa realized she should check in with her sister. Grant hadn't any obligations.

The two of them agreed on the impulse: get out of town.

***

Twenty-two hours later, they were in Taos, searching for food.

"What do you suggest?" asked Grant, eyeing the Orlando's waitress who wore a revealing shirt, one with ends she had tied it together at her waist. Marissa studied Grant.

"Shrimp enchiladas are the best," the waitress said. "Hot, if you know what I mean." She squirmed and fiddled with her outfit.

Grant reddened while Marissa stood. "I need a minute," she said and walked away.

The waitress, now tugging at both ends of her top, stood in front of Grant, who tried to look away. She turned sideways and raised her upper body.

"Look, I don't know what you're thinking, but obviously"—he gestured over his shoulder toward Marissa—"I'm not in any position... I mean, I don't want to, either."

The waitress smiled and walked away as Marissa returned.

"I saw the way you were looking at her. If I were a guy, I would do the same," she said.

"Sorry. She practically shoved her chest in my face," he said.

Marissa laughed. Why should she care, so soon, about this new man? But she had discovered, more than once, that what she was feeling wasn't an intellectual choice. If she wanted a guy, she would be jealous every time he even glanced at someone else. No disclaimers worked.

"I feel secure about what I have," she said.

"You should, and I am sorry I said that," Grant replied, getting down on one knee as he grabbed a flower from a nearby vase. "Forgive me?"

"It's not like we're a couple. We just met," she said.

"True, but, ever the romantic, I'm hoping maybe there's more to come?" he asked. "Either I haven't been around or I just haven't run into someone like you: blunt, funny, out there. Sexy, too."

"Yeah, really," she said, repositioning her shirt.

"Maybe we ought to get out of here," Grant said.

"But we just got here." She looked at him and reconsidered. "You could be right." She paused. "I feel like a fifteen-year-old about to sneak out with a cool boy I'm not supposed to be with."

Grant took her by the hand and eased her out of her chair just as the waitress returned with waters. She knew.

"Don't," said Grant as he took out a ten-dollar bill and handed it to the young woman. She took it, stuffed it down the front of her revealing red bra, and spun away.

He opened the door of the Corolla for Marissa. While she was settling in and pulling her seat belt into place, he leaned over and kissed her on the lips. She unlatched herself and grabbed the light brown hair which fell toward his shoulders.

Marissa was, against her will, drawn to him. It didn't much matter whether she liked or wanted this. She'd had enough of boys and men. When she was thirteen and already growing, she had tried to hide her body by hunching over, but it didn't work. Adolescent boys, after all, had both eyes and imaginations. Initially, she was curious. Why not?

She now tried to assess a man before committing to any type of relationship. Grant, though, had her at hello and she could not say no.

"Ever been to the Grant Canyon?" he asked.

"Funny. Actually, no. Commercial, isn't it? Why? You interested?" She paused, then added, "I do like cowboys," and instantly regretted having said so.

"I pull a mean trigger, but only on one of those fake kid guns," said Grant.

"You don't have to try so hard, Grant. For whatever reason, I'm with you."

"Thanks. I think we ought to go to the canyon. I've never been, either," he said.

"Why not? Driving around with you is . . ." she could not think of a word or phrase to describe it.

Drive he did. Marissa, feeling her eyes closing, struggled to keep awake. Everything around her was a shade of red: crimson, maroon, rust, and ruby. The mountains seemed flushed, deepening into rouge components as the sun set. She dreamt as she napped and Grant went up and around, up and around. She felt the swirl, but it wasn't annoying. Rather, this rocked Marissa to sleep.

She dreamt of growing up in New Jersey. Marissa wanted to be a cheerleader and she had the voice to do it, but she was shy. Not of the routines; it was her body holding her back, even then. Developing too early made it awkward. She could not imagine jostling around in front of hundreds of people. So she tried out her jumps and spins and cheers for her little sister, Diana. Marissa wished they could have traded bodies, just for six months, so that cheerleading would have been a go.

Marissa felt the sway of the car as Grant navigated the turns of the mountains. Falling in and out of reverie, she wanted to slide beside Grant, lean on him, but this car didn't permit that. She thought she remembered that when she was little, the family car—it was old, like a Plymouth—had a bench seat in the front. Sometimes, she and Diana used to squish in between their parents, all four of them sitting in the front. Other times, the sisters stayed in the back—and just as well. There, they could create games and their own little world, leaving the serious matters to the adults in the front.

The car lurched forward, and Marissa snapped toward the passenger door, her seatbelt restraining her.

"Sorry! Something ran out," Grant said. "I don't know what it was. Do they have foxes around here?"

"You're asking the wrong person, but isn't this coyote or wolf country? As in Wiley?"

"A woman after my own heart—one who watched cartoons when she was a little girl," said Grant.

Marissa did not want to talk. He drove, relying on his primitive GPS for directions. He had an early version of the technology but trusted the device. When driving and uncertain of her whereabouts, Marissa wished neither to ask for directions nor to consult maps. On occasion, she would rather remain lost. Was this truly a better idea than a voice-driven locator?

Grant found Diana Krall through the Sirius service the rental provided. Marissa listened to "Fly Me to the Moon," followed by a highly romantic version of "Just the Way You Are."

"Marissa." Grant stated her name. She had been dozing off now and again until Grant stopped the car, reached over, and smoothed her hair.

"What?"

"Georgia O'Keeffe," he said.

"My English teacher in high school, Mr. B, told us all about her—Stieglitz, the painting, the pictures, the love story, the Southwest."

"Well, that's exactly it, Marissa. We could find O'Keeffe," he said.

It was still Diana Krall on the radio, and Marissa wondered if Krall and O'Keeffe had much in common. Sensuous, artistic sensibility . . .

Grant interrupted her thoughts by saying, "That must have been one hot relationship." He paused. "I mean Stieglitz and O'Keeffe."

"I know what you're talking about, and that's one way to describe it. I will say that."

"Look at her and imagine what he was seeing through the lens," he said.

Grant took her hand and kissed it.

Marissa blushed—and then grabbed him and hugged him as hard as she could. For some reason, she wondered if O'Keeffe and Krall had been contemporaries, would they have been friends or more than that?

Marissa knew she was falling for Grant, but they'd just met. She told herself to resist the impulse, but would she? Soon she snuggled into him and realized she would not let go, not now.

Grant lifted her thick brown hair in order to place his hand at the top of her spinal column. He let it rest there and, ever so gently, touched her.

Marissa held onto him and said, "I just want to take you home with me, and I appear to be a Brooklynite." She paused. "Hopeless romantic I am, like Diana Krall. I mean her music, not her, I suppose, but I don't know."

She could feel Grant's smile.

She could see Georgia O'Keeffe.

Landscape, Stieglitz, portrait.

O'Keeffe. Diana Krall sings Georgia O'Keeffe.

Marissa thought, just perhaps, Grant would be the guy.

Chapter 4

Sheffield, Massachusetts

mid-July 2010

MARISSA WAS AFRAID TO ask him if it was the sex. Why else, soon after they'd come together, would he follow her to this town where she was scheduled to do a theater workshop? What more could be in it for him? They had managed to survive on savings and occasional part-time jobs, and Marissa chose not to do the play in Alphabet City. Working for real money should be the top priority. It was 5:00 a.m., and they had arrived the previous day, found the B&B, settled in, and here she was—pondering. The violet pre-dawn sky featured deep orange highlights as the sun announced its presence. Staring, she felt at peace but understood that this was ephemeral. She wanted Grant to wake up so they could share the view, one she expected would never be hers again. She grabbed an old pair of jeans and a sweater and made her way down the stairs and out the back door. Plopping down in a green Adirondack chair, Marissa was surprised when she heard the screen door open behind her. Turning her head, she saw Grant standing there.

He sat on an arm of the chair at first, then slid, awkwardly, into Marissa's lap.

Neither spoke as an early morning cardinal danced toward them.

"Just a dancer who belongs way up there in the sky," whispered Grant. Marissa, while nodding, cradled his head, took in his scent, and slumped back down in the chair.

"Grant, I'm here to audition. Well, they asked me to come, so maybe I'm in something and it's just a matter of finding out what at this point. About you, though . . . This thing, whatever it is, that I want to continue to happen . . . well . . ."

"It's rare that someone sweeps me completely off my feet," he said. "I savor that. The rest? Give me a few days and I'll figure it out."

"I might love you enough to marry you someday," said Marissa.

"Marriage, wow, but sure or probably sure," said Grant.

"Now, I have to shower and compose myself for theater." She kissed him on the mouth, and he stared upward as the sky bequeathed an early morning tone of blue.

They had chosen a place within walking distance of the high school that the theater company was operating out of. Marissa, given the choice between driving the rental car or making her way on foot, chose option two, thinking it may offer time for her to practice her version of meditation. Walking along the side of the road, she realized she would rather turn around and spend the day with Grant, but she also wanted to be part of this new play festival and had been thrilled when she received word that they looked forward to seeing her. In a short while, she imagined, someone would hand her a script and possibly give her a part, and then she would instantly become part of a new community. Only the allure of this man could distract her. As she made the short trek, she put time with him on the agenda for much later that day, that night. Grant was a patient human, one who would wait.

For years, a prestigious theater company had often made Mt. Everett High School its temporary home over the summer. Marissa had seen *A Little Night Music* there and *Company*, both enthralling Sondheim musicals. She adored Sondheim. The professional troupe had moved on and relocated a number of miles to the north. To her knowledge, the current residential group was local and non-Equity. This was fine.

The small hand-painted sign poised on the edge of the main drag said, "SST—Follow Me," and Marissa knew this meant Sheffield Summer Theater. She turned up the long driveway and briskly walked toward the main entrance of the building, which was already adorned with a sweet logo and snappy sign. As she pulled the door open, she convinced herself that this was her place for now. Any ambivalence resolved immediately as two happy people greeted her and then escorted her into the lobby.

"I bet this is Marissa," said a guy with a droopy mustache and, perhaps in contradiction, perfectly combed hair.

"What a beautiful name," said a genuinely beautiful woman whose age Marissa could not determine. She could be eighteen or she could be thirty-one.

"Yes, I'm Marissa, but I am not so sure about my name. It's just what people call me. Did either of you ever think about changing yours?"

"Sorry. I'm Mal, and this is Syd," said the man. "We're cowriting a play and, well, we want you in it."

"But you don't know who I am," said Marissa. "Right?"

Syd answered the question: "Marissa, for Mal and for me, the workshop gives us a chance to hear and watch our script come to life. So we were careful to invite people here whom we think will fit and who will love this opportunity. We were impressed with the tape you sent. We're eager to hear you read."

Trying to block out any thought of Grant, Marissa focused on Syd's words. "Thank you so much," she said. "Could be I've been looking for you, too."

"Come to the theater, Marissa," said Mal, pulling her along.

She had been here and recalled the production photos, head shots, and playbills that were mounted and framed on the walls. Most of the year, it was still a high school building, complete with sports banners, a *Chorus Line* poster, and a teacher-of-the-month notation.

Mal was moving rapidly, while Marissa and Syd had to double time it to keep up. Marissa heard laughter before entering the auditorium. When she did, everything stopped.

A young woman with red hair piled on her head shouted from the stage, "Marissa, yay!" Marissa smiled and waved. Several people sat, every which way, on or beneath the stage apron—on chairs, on the floor, on steps positioned far to the right or left. It seemed, to Marissa, that, on cue, everyone looked at her and everyone seemed excited to see her. She was thrilled to be there.

"I'm Katie C. because we have another Katie, over there," the red-haired woman said while a young woman with blue-black hair waved. "Some call me KC to make it easy, and I don't mind."

Mal signaled for Marissa to follow him down the aisle, and Syd went to sit with everyone else.

"Marissa, we've been saving a monologue for you," Mal said when they reached the foot of the stage. "I know this is sudden, but could you try it? We all know a cold reading can be tough, but we've been anticipating your arrival. Okay?"

Syd, a woman who seemed to choose her words carefully, spoke. "I apologize for throwing this at you, Marissa," she said, "but we're hopeful that it works for you."

"Of course, yes," she said. "But can you give me some plot and context?"

"The scene is an abandoned country house here in the Berkshires or, for that matter, the Catskills. We haven't become specific. It's the day before a wedding and, really, some kind of awakening. An attractive young woman—Lenore—walks into a wooded area. She will see her fiancé soon." Syd paused to look at Marissa, who nodded, so she continued, "Thank you, again, Marissa. Lenore was in and out of neighborhoods and, suddenly, she was not. Instead, she was walking on a gentle uphill and saw a building at the crest."

Mal jumped in. "Up she goes, unable to resist the impulse to explore even though she knows this might not be wise. Thus, the monologue." He handed her a script that was open to the appropriate page.

Marissa made her way up the stairs. Before saying a word, she walked to the center of the stage and, as she had been instructed years ago, took three steps forward. She wondered whether she should find that spot above the rear wall, as a high school drama instructor had once advised, or go with her instincts. She ended up focusing on a young man with a day's growth of beard and a green baseball cap. He was seated several rows deep in a center seat. Marissa, imagining light shining in her eyes, spoke to him as

Lenore:

"Alone but not afraid. This is my mantra. I was only eight years old when the little boy who lived next door did what everyone said never to do: run into the street to fetch a pink rubber ball. And the bus, which seemed enormous to me at the time even though it was a regular bus, which smelled of gasoline, lurched backward and into Robert, killing him. I stared at this and was shaken, well, forever. Six months later, his mother hanged herself. I carried with me this picture I created of Mrs. Harrison dangling from a basement overhanging support because we had them and I couldn't imagine how else she might have done it. Everyone was so hush-hush quiet about it. No one said a word, and when they did, they lied. Mrs. Harrison, even before, seemed terribly unhappy and now she was at peace—maybe even with Robert. They would be relieved to be reunited. But I was just eight and did not know what to think. This probably marked my first retreat from reality.

"I was able to mask it well enough. I lived in my room as often as possible. The walls were painted white, and I found a kind of chalk I could use for drawing or writing on them that would wash right off. After a while, the white became muddier and I was glad to paint over it. Whatever pleased my parents, those people who seemed to get along so well. They were the best community theater actors around."

Here, Marissa paused to catch her breath and slow down. She looked over at Syd, who nodded.

"In fact, I remember them in *Kiss Me Kate*," she continued, "as a couple at war yet playful. I guess I was able to create a fantasy world all my own since my little brother would not come along for almost ten years. My childhood was open for my imagination. I would write stories on my wall, and I would be the star: the girl who grew up to marry the handsome prince or, well, whatever he would be. That would shift. Sometimes, I would become an outstanding speaker or the best swimmer. It was fun, but in secret, I was remembering the bus and wondering where Robert went."

Marissa moved a few steps to her left and raised her eyes. She thought about asking for a break, then quickly resumed the reading:

"This went on for quite some time. On the surface, I was a dreamy little girl who was growing up and could dance and sing. I guess everyone knew that I was painting pictures on the bedroom walls, but the writings I always erased before they could be viewed. These were private, but with my Kodak camera, I was able to record much of what I was saying. I think I was writing prose poems before I even knew of such a category.

Alien texture finely sculpted
angel
on the wheel
Thrown by a novice craftsman
who
should make
movies
epic, three-hour visual extravaganzas:
love/war morality films set amid raging
forest fires
Save Me!

Yes, it was my way of reaching out when I was approaching adolescence as a precocious thirteen- or fourteen-year-old awaiting a woman's body."

Marissa stopped again. Mal walked toward her, but she waved him off and continued:

"I had a partial view and heard what happened—the awful, awesome truth. He was gone, and I did not move on. I mean, I did continue to go to school. My room, though, became more and more of a haven. The walls were like a precursor to smart boards. My version was more primitive but just as effective. Now, though, I think about what I lost. I did have the pictures and would provide words which would become memoir material. Maybe my nightmares had me under those massive wheels. Unimaginable. Instead, I hear the noise as Robert did. This is the moment I fear."

Marissa sat down on the stage floor as tears streamed down her cheeks. Then her cell phone, which she had forgotten to silence, went off. It was Grant. She ignored the call and turned off the ring tone, but her thoughts flew to him. She stood and stared at the rear wall, and there he was, walking down the aisle looking directly at her. Marissa was newly part of the group now even if her interactions with them had been limited. So far, all that had really happened was that she had been thrown this monologue with the trust that she could deliver. She needed to get back to the passage and, as she had learned years before, block out the rest—including her lover's smile and scent.

"Marissa, amazing cold reading," said Mal.

"Truly moving," added Syd. "We knew you would be the fit. Let's take a break."

Overwhelmed, Marissa nodded and then slid off the front of the stage and found Grant, who embraced her.

"You don't mind that I found my way here?" he asked.

"No, but how did you do it?"

"The name of the high school was written on a scratch pad you left in the B&B. I figured out the rest."

Mal and Syd came to greet them while the others dispersed.

"Mal, Syd, this is Grant. He's my boyfriend," said Marissa. "Do you mind if we talk for a few minutes before we all get together?"

"We threw you into the monologue headfirst, Marissa. Take an extra ten minutes, please," said Syd.

Marissa's mind raced through the past few months: the time in the Southwest, coupling with Grant, one night at the B&B, the monologue. How could she process all of it when she now had eight minutes and counting?

"Grant, walk with me."

They made their way out the front door and headed around the building. Marissa saw a trail leading into the woods but realized there wasn't any time to take it.

"Stay and watch," she said.

Grant replied, "Yes. I definitely want to watch the process, see you act, your passion. Let's go back inside."

She hooked her arm through his and, with fingers intertwined, they entered the building and then the auditorium.

Marissa was ready to resume the monologue:

"Looking back, I recall that evening as launching my end-of-life obsession . . . and the dreams include visions, darkness."

Marissa felt the words and her vulnerability. For a moment, she forgot who she was—Lenore or Marissa. Of course, she knew the answer but it was all coming so very close. Why? She did not have a haunting Robert in her past—at least, not that she could remember. Here she was, though, welling up once again. The character, the writing, the painting she visualized on the girl's walls—this was totally intimate and might as well have been her own story. Such a swirl of activity, hard for her to sort though. She saw Grant, with that old Hollywood smile, searching for eye contact.

Mal was beside her on the stage and looking straight into her eyes.

"Marissa, you are amazing. We are so, so lucky to have you here, doing this with us."

Marissa looked at Mal and then at Grant, who was still smiling. She began to relax.

"Maybe we should move on to something else," Mal suggested. "We can come back to the monologue later."

"I can do it if you want. Just needed a breather," Marissa said.

"There's no question you are our Lenore. Rest assured. Take a bit more time."

As Marissa walked down the steps, several in the hall clapped and someone simply said, "Marissa." She didn't recall ever feeling this valued as an actor before.

Grant embraced her, sweetly overwhelming Marissa with his hug, and she collapsed into him. Off they went back into the summer Berkshire sunlight. She flashed upon her theater moments in high school—especially the time she played Ophelia. Marissa realized her mother, too, had that role. She knew that no one thought she could do it; neither did she — this was a pattern. It was a time when she knew she had to become thinner. Marissa, contours and all, decided that Ophelia, going mad, needed to look stressed and scratchy. It wasn't the director's call, but he did not argue. Now, though, she looked like, well, herself.

"I can see how badly you need this, Marissa," said Grant. "I knew acting was an interest of yours, but now I see your passion, which absolutely becomes you."

Marissa loved listening to this man speak. He was articulate, even eloquent. She tightened her grip around his waist and wondered if he might fit the clichéd yet desired description of Mr. Right.

Her head, though, was thinking of Lenore and those words. Marissa needed to get back inside the hall. Grant was a willing collaborator.

She was now at ease as she greeted new theater friends. She counted roughly a dozen people in the room. A bear of a man tossed out his hand as she passed by. "My name is Donald. Everyone calls me Rudy. Don't ask, but I promise to tell you the story."

Syd was on stage. "Well, we really didn't introduce Marissa, which was not kind to her. I did tell her how we all anticipated, with great expectations, her arrival. Those hopes have been met, yes?"

Clapping followed, along with some cheers and woo hoo's.

"Let's get back to it, and then Mal and I will relax and quit dominating this day," Syd added.

Marissa, feeling more comfortable, took a longer route to the stage, circling the seats. It was a technique she had discovered years before as a way to maintain her composure. She mused upon, once again, the time in Moab—meeting Grant; leaving her sister and that boyfriend she shouldn't have; and the sweet, speedy Southwest tour. She was stoked to receive the invitation to come to Sheffield. Here they were, and she was at the foot of the stage.

"Before I continue, let me just say many thanks to all of you," Marissa said. "This is insane, but you have accepted me even though you don't really know me. Later, I want to get to know each person here."

Beginning to feel the voice of her character, Marissa continued to read from the script:

"I am fifteen; I am not certain. Becoming a woman is different from actually being a woman. No, that doesn't really sound right. Could I please skip to the next phase, pass through 'becoming' and reach 'is'? My skin is literally expanding and, oppositional to everything I heard, I like growing up a bit. I was less comfortable as a girl than as this adolescent. Maybe that's because my childhood was spent so often within the confines of my house and my side yard. We did not have a backyard but one and a half lots. I know: a mystery. We also had six-foot hedges acting as a barrier. I liked being by myself and was not especially sociable. These mid-teens somehow allow me to become more confident instead of fearful. Boys notice me, and I am supposed to be outraged but I feel flattered. Remember that I was the little girl who had created a cocoon around her to protect and save herself."

As she read, Marissa tried to distinguish between Lenore and herself. She did not grow up in isolation. She and Diana were close sisters for a good while. Then they went their separate ways as they forged individual identities. It all seemed normal, but the monologue was striking chords within her, some of which were off pitch.

She saw Mal and Syd gathering and wondered if she, suddenly, had lost the thread or, worse, their belief.

Mal spoke first: "Marissa, it's great. Not to worry. Your delivery is moving. Syd and I need to go back to work on it. You've helped us to see that. It's too something or other. What is it, Syd?"

"Like a social psychology essay on a young woman's coming of age. And, to be sure, that is part of what we want. But we are preaching too often and, thanks to you, Marissa, Mal and I are closely listening," said Syd. "So, we can retire this monologue for a little while. Give us time to tinker with it and go back to the overall dialogue in the script," she added.

"Should I take a short break, or would it be better if I stayed?" asked Marissa.

Mal and Syd exchanged a glance. It was clear they had worked together for some time.

"We are doing as much as possible during a given day," said Mal. "Marissa, if you feel up to it, come see us after you and your fellow get some dinner."

Marissa, relieved, smiled and quickly walked over to Grant, who put his arm, gently, around her shoulders. They walked out of the building and down the windy road toward the B&B.

"I didn't know that you could be both serious and good at the same time," said Grant.

"What?"

"Acting, performing, being on stage—all of that," he said.

"Grant, high school theater kept me going for a long time. It gave me license to be someone else on stage. It is everything: high-risk, total pressure, sweet reward, and then, each time, elation and deflation as a production closes. Besides, everything in the New York City suburbs is competitive. Did you ever act in a show?"

"I did. I was a member of the jury in *Twelve Angry Men*. I was the last one to see that the guy being tried was not guilty."

"You're not at all like that character," she said. "You're a listener, and that is rare. So what was it like for you to be the most obstinate juror?"

"Well, it was fun for sure. And hard, too. I didn't like him, so I made up my mind that his inner nature was really better than that." He paused. "What about you? Which role stays with you the most?"

"When I was fourteen, I was cast as Juliet in a community theater production. It was an honor, and I changed my entire look for that role."

"I love your look, Marissa," said Grant.

"I was young and I was developing, and, well, I just assumed they would take someone who was flat-chested."

"Was the Romeo knock-out handsome?"

"He was four or five years older than me but looked sixteen, and he was fair and blond."

"And?"

"He had these perfect features that I found too smooth, too symmetrical. It wasn't his fault and I certainly didn't mind embracing him, but there wasn't any magnetic attraction. Nothing of that sort."

"I'm already jealous," said Grant.

Marissa laughed. "I never did go for Prince Charming. You don't need to worry."

"So you're saying I am not especially good looking."

Marissa ignored the comment, "Let me ask you, then, what do you look for in a woman?"

"Personality combined with physical. No, that's lame. You. I've been looking for you."

Waves of heat and increasing humidity encased them as they walked. Midsummer days in the Berkshires were never ending. Sunlight bathed them even during late afternoon, and they held each other as if to make certain they would never part. It had not rained in days, and even the most minor gust of wind kicked up sand and grit and beige dust from the dirt road. Marissa waved away that scrim-like mixture when, seemingly without care or precaution or awareness, several deer appeared, cavorted across the path, and bounded into the forest on the other side. Marissa grabbed at Grant but missed his arm. He stopped, gripped her hand, and stared.

"Yes. Physical touch is okay. In my youth, and even more recently, I feared this."

"Like Lenore remembering Robert or something like that?" Grant asked.

"Grant, Lenore was terrified of somehow becoming a Robert even when she was years older. I once resisted touch because it was coming to me too early," said Marissa.

The deer were lingering just ahead of them. Marissa tiptoed toward them, still holding onto Grant's hand. She whispered, "I wish I could pet one of them."

Grant placed his index finger over her lips to shush her.

A doe danced forward. Marissa extended her palm, and the deer neither advanced nor retreated. It seemed to Marissa that the animal was staring squarely at her and, she imagined, thinking about her. Then it walked toward the others but looked back, all the while, at Marissa.

"I'm more a set person," said Grant. "To me, this does seem to all be part of a production: the monologue, this deer. Or maybe it's more like a film awaiting its dramatic plot turn. That was a great interaction. What happens next?"

"So true. It's hard for me to process—like someone is writing a script for us," said Marissa. "Anyway, let's get dinner before I have to go to rehearsal." She moved forward by herself, gently detaching from Grant, who was comfortable staying several paces behind. He turned to the woods and began to speak.

"Call this my monologue," he began as Marissa stopped, turned, and listened. "Or call it, if you would rather, Ode to Marissa. First line: I am drop-dead smitten with you as we enjoy our anniversary. We've been together two months, my dear. Even if it sounds dumb, naive, this is true."

"Grant," said Marissa. "I think . . . I might . . . I can love you. Here is my run-on story. I have five minutes before needing to reappear inside. Listen:

"I was born when my parents were living in Brooklyn Heights. They were Ethical Culture, then Unitarian. Never was my mother in denial of her Hebraic heritage. Nor did either of them suggest, except for once, that I tend to religion. On my father's side, his own mother was a Russian Jew and his father a Quaker. It's no wonder, you might say, that I am a hybrid. I see myself, at least, as immensely spiritual. Not a Sunday morning attendee.

"They, my parents, were often together. An attorney first before she became a guidance counselor, she had an office attached to our home, with nonprofits as clients.

And my dad did some graphic design as a side profession. He would work for someone for a while, then set up his own business and repeat that formula, always somehow able to contribute to our family's financial needs. You know, he was like a master of many trades, writer or journalist. He made signs: a big salami; a paper company; Pizza Plus; electronics repair; clothing boutique. When he had work, he was happy. When he did not, he sat in his basement studio and sketched. But, no matter what anyone said, Dad felt he let us down.

"I listened to jazz, mostly on the radio, and tried to improvise on piano. Took lessons from the time I was eight. Not interested, I nonetheless absorbed the basics: geography of the keyboard, rhythms.

I played my electronic keyboard, began creating, composing, and wondered if it was the start of a career. The coffeehouse at nearby Unitarian Church became my spot. My parents floated in and out of the liberal religions, but I stayed—not on Sunday mornings, except later, when I was asked to play mostly on Friday nights."

Grant responded with, "I had only one serious girlfriend, whom I convinced myself I would marry. Tall and willowy and a scientist—a future physicist. In the end, her constant analysis of herself, and of me, caused some distance. She thought about the past and present while prognosticating the future. You, though, are very much an in-the-moment human being. Is this your theater training? You know me: I attempt to go with the flow even as I shield my own anxieties."

"Grant, this is more than wonderful, but what are we doing?" asked Marissa.

Startled, he grasped for her. "I have never really shared that with anyone," he said. "I mean, I've been writing it forever—well, since last year. Not that this is what I planned. I've been composing songs, yes, but not a narrative. Sorry."

"Don't be. I have never been able to play myself very well—until the past few weeks. I know that's gushing, but it's true." She stopped and looked into his eyes. "Soon I go back in there, separate out the personal from this individual who maybe visualizes herself on stage."

"Marissa, I just watched you become Lenore. It is your time. This—I mean, the stage—is where you should be," he said. "Like the deer. You brighten on the stage even when the script is filled with trepidation and sadness for you, your character. I mean it, Marissa."

"It's a lot at once for me to consider. I would pretty much go anywhere with you, Grant. Maybe not back to the Southwest right off. I want to treasure that scene from the beginning of the romance."

"It was kind of charged," he said.

Marissa blushed.

"You are one passionate woman," said Grant. "No one else is here. You had me without even saying hello, Marissa."

"In a few years, we'll return. You're making me long for a bed."

"Sorry for being a man," he said. "I could add more."

"I get it," said Marissa.

Marissa's rehearsal break was late for dinner, but it was still light. They ambled along the dusty tamped-down trail alongside the road until, at a corner, they noticed a sign that read "Leftover Veggies: Free or Leave Some Change." Marissa pulled out three dollar bills, placed them beneath a zucchini, and grabbed some ripe, luscious-looking tomatoes. Grant picked up some carrots and said, "All we need is a baguette and a bottle of red wine."

"Might have to make do without those, or at least until later—way later," said Marissa.

So they sat and ate. Marissa remembered that she had a water bottle in the side pocket of her backpack. "Cheers," she said before taking a sip and passing it to Grant.

"Kind of like Utah without the red rocks," he remarked. "Where would you rather live—the Southwest or here?"

"Grant, we've only been here a couple of days."

"You told me you went to summer camp nearby," said Grant. "And now I will let out this not-so-secret secret: I used to spend a couple of weeks each summer a few hills over learning how to hit a backhand."

"That is not a side of you I saw in the Southwest or now. Music, yes; this, no. Next thing you will tell me is that you were on an athletic scholarship," said Marissa.

"Not. I went to Skidmore thinking music. For the first two years, I did swat a few tennis balls. When the push came to actually play in matches, I said no. I think certain people wish I were on the sports grant. Grant. Get it?"

"I know about theater there, at Skidmore," said Marissa. "I did a workshop with SITI Company there. You wouldn't know who they are. I got to meet an actor—I think it was Tom Hewitt—and then he was on Broadway in *Rocky Horror*. Grant, I think I have to get back to the theater for the evening run. Is that okay?"

"Of course. Tell me about SITI sometime. I didn't expect to pry you away at all. Just came to watch. I don't have to stay, Marissa. What's better for you?"

"Stay. Watch and listen. Please."

She took his hand to stand and linked his arm as they walked back at a brisker pace. Marissa saw one star in the slightly darkening sky above the roof of the high school building and then they were back.

"Marissa," said Mal. "Welcome once again. Are you ready?"

"Yes, for the monologue. I want this, but I took the time to rest instead of study. I hope that's okay."

"You got hit with all of this at once, so we know it's a lot to take in," said Mal.

Marissa hopped onto the stage and skidded to her landing.

Laughing, Marissa said, mostly to herself, "Lenore, where are you?" before turning to the pages:

"Sixteen is different. I'm not fearful, not nearly so. I don't know why, but it's also not for me to question. What happened to Robert will not happen to me. I will climb and swim and skate. New challenges replace what kept me stuck in place like a retractable rubber band. I tried pushing, but it would smack back. Now I know I need to play on since that makes me invulnerable, doesn't it? Boys are noticing me, bumping into me, and pretending the touching is accidental. My feelings about this are mixed. Sure, it's awful. Still, this makes me feel desired. Oh really, you ask? Masking my insecurities was, for me, survival."

Mal interjected, "I will read for Henry, Marissa, who was Lenore's first boyfriend. You have the script with an extended monologue for her, but let's edit out the rest. Try it for now and we can always put it back in later."

"Fine with me," said Marissa. "Honestly, I'm relieved."

"First, though, maybe we all should just sit for a minute and talk," said Mal. "You've been jettisoned right into the middle of all this, Marissa."

With that, a group of actors, set designers, and others associated with the production made their way to the front of the stage. All seemed to be talking—to one another, to themselves . . .

Marissa laughed—at first softly to herself, and then more broadly. Syd joined in and, lifting her arms toward both her friends and the ceiling, encouraged everyone to do the same. The actors, happily alerted, embellished guffaws, howls, and deep-throated roars.

"Welcome to South County Theater, Marissa. You rock," said Syd. "You shine with skills, and you are endearing. You glow,"

Beaming, Marissa said, "You guys are so kind to have me. Do I feel the pressure? Yeah, a little bit. I feel like it's showtime, that's all. That is where I want to be, just as I want to be right here, right now. When do I get my counseling session on which restaurants are five stars without the fancy prices, though?"

"AJ can help you with that," said Mal. "You can see why."

Marissa had neither met nor heard of AJ.

He came around from the rear of the stage, sporting a mass of curly hair, a beard, jean shorts, and heavy work boots. "I'm the TD, Marissa," he said in a soothing voice that did not match his physique. "At your service and glad to have you."

Marissa, loving his phrasing, said, "AJ, I'm pleased."

He bowed deeply and slowly, all of his hair leading him downward. It was a highly dramatic moment, and, to her amazement, it emanated from the vital tech man rather than one of the many performers.

Then a violently loud whack sounded as if an earthquake were shaking the building and the grounds.

"What's that?" yelled Syd nervously.

"Calm yourselves," said AJ in a deep baritone. "It's summertime." He smiled broadly, and Marissa thought of his potential as an actor. Naturally poised and literally a huge presence. "Come on, everyone," he implored. "Outside for the spectacular."

All followed as AJ, facilitating, spread his arms toward a kaleidoscopic sky.

Purple, indigo, and wild orange-gold threads blasted through the clouds. Marissa put her hand up to create a shield for her face, because it was torrentially raining as well. AJ wanted his friends to experience the technicolor deluge through feel. "Sense memory," he chanted, even if that was an improper call. The exhilarating, welcoming chords were striking, and some joined in.

A rain dance followed: Theater people, she thought, were warped or, more precisely, caught in that hippiedom time zone. Gyrations, spins, handstands, and sensuous bumps amid the driving raindrops!

"God, listen to us. Watch us!" someone yelled.

"Bliss is ignorance!" Mal called.

"Let's sing to the rain dance, too," said Syd.

It wasn't even organized chaos: soaked twenty- and thirty-somethings running in circles, zigs, and zags, both at one another and away from one another.

"Can I do the monologue out here?" asked Marissa.

"Speak it," said AJ.

Realizing she didn't have the script and would lose the moment if she went back inside to track it down, Marissa decided to improvise. "I'm not Robert," she said. "I refuse to be paralyzed by the thought of an improbable incident. Let me be free! Let me fly out of that trap!" she called. "For he never had the opportunity to question, to wonder whether it was all worth it: at age five or six, then everything that followed. Upward swirls and downward spirals." Marissa stopped and snapped the fingers of her right hand. "Find it now, not the next day. Tomorrow will be too late! Late! Late!" until others joined her. "Find it now," was the group cry. Her new friends caught the raindrops or at least attempted to do as much by cupping their hands. The results were marginally successful, and the process a neat blend of ingenuity and hilarity.

Chapter 5

Provincetown, Massachusetts

late August 2010

MARISSA FELT AS IF her sweat had permeated all within sight: sticking to the furniture, the walls, the ceiling. Tropical mugginess: the heat wave brought out gnats and little creatures she did not even realize existed. After the performance, she and Grant had decided to come here for a week, by themselves. The Berkshires experience was sensational for the acting troupe, and Grant was a mensch for putting up with it. But now she wanted quiet—and him. The view from the tiny rental, which they called Shack, showed Commercial Street and the bay beyond—the west side of town between the tourist trap and, further up, North Truro. Inside, she felt safe within the snug confines even as sauntering passersby came oh so close to her window.

She was learning to be a morning person, realizing Grant often beamed between sunrise and noon. The morning light seemed to infuse him with charismatic volts of current. When the late summer sun retired for the night, so did he. Not that she minded mellow, but it was thrilling for her to be caught up in the morning charge.

"What if we could sip coffee, make love, and catch the buzz of this town?" he asked.

"I want to be in the movies," said Marissa. "Is that possible? For me? For you?"

"You know the story: It's all about being in the right place at the right time," said Grant.

"You forgot about the part when I fall for the sweetest, most alluring guy I ever met."

He smiled and said, "You got me."

"We're a continent away from Moab," said Marissa.

"We're not that far, in spirit, when you think about it. The main difference is the color of the trees and, well, the garnet rocks out there."

"I grew up with green," she said. "Let's go back to the Southwest. Try rafting, climbing, and whatever else Moab compels us to do."

"You sound like an actor. Is that your motivation—physical risk?" he asked.

"It's where we met, and maybe I am in love because of, well, Arches? Although I'm afraid of heights and not exactly the athlete," she said.

"Not yet," said Grant. "We're in P-town for now and have plenty of time to work our way to Moab."

He took her hand, lifted her up gently, and said, "It's still early in the morning. Let's just stroll the streets." Grant put on a hat, his girlfriend having advised him that the sun could burn, and led Marissa toward the front door of their motel room.

. "Voila," he said, opening the door of the sweet room and pointing across the street toward the bay beyond.

"I accept," she answered. "Provincetown it is for now, and perhaps later Moab?" she asked.

"That's an enthusiastic yes from me. I've been here more often than you, so I will lead if you will follow," said Grant. With that, he coaxed her to the opposite side of the road, with its bay view. "It changes color maybe twenty-five or thirty feet out. It's a deep, almost purple, blue, and it will turn to black tonight," he said.

He was tempted to suggest that they wade in but then opted for a long walk toward North Truro, away from the P-town hubbub and along the gently winding shore, then inland as the tide was hundreds of yards out. A large and friendly-looking Labrador Retriever seemed to be skimming the surface as the dog raced toward lobster traps. Marissa wondered what would happen if it caught up. She loved lobster—dead lobster, that is; she was terrified that, when alive, the rambunctious shellfish could ensnare all beings, including her, within their claws. The fleet-footed canine screeched to a halt at the lobster nets, then began sniffing furiously while maintaining a few inches of distance between its nose and the snappers.

"Whoa," said Grant, and Marissa wondered if this word was a remnant from his Moab days.

"You really are a cowboy—a sophisticated, caring, eye-catching, sexy cowboy," she said.

"Glad you tossed in sexy at the end, babe," he answered.

"Babe, huh? But do you think I could stand to lose a few pounds?"

"No. That's the short answer. I could say more, but that might cause trouble."

"Let's run," said Marissa. She jogged after the retreating black dog, whose muzzle was draped in wet, limp seaweed. Her long-legged, lanky boyfriend hadn't any trouble keeping up. She liked watching his flying hair, which seemed to sprout wings along his temples and behind his head. He was a lopper but an upright one. Marissa ran with her softly curled fists in front of her chest. With Grant, she was not self-conscious. Soon, the retriever, giving up the game, came to them.

"Tell us about your day," said Marissa to the dog, which shook hard enough to spray both of the onlookers.

"Nice and refreshing," said Grant.

The Lab jumped up and licked Grant's face before turning to Marissa. On hind legs, the black dog stood eyeball to eyeball with her and seemed to smile right at her.

"I'll take that," she said. "Now where are your owners or parents?"

With that, the animal shook free and, once again, showered anyone nearby with saltwater. Then, with a turn toward the shore, the dog indicated where it belonged.

"Let's walk back with this sweet one," said Marissa as Grant nodded. Even though the dog seemed to know where it belonged, Marissa couldn't say the same. "I sort of don't know where I belong, Grant."

"On my elbow seems right to me," he said.

"Right, yes. I mean in life. The Southwest seemed perfect until the Berkshires and now here. I like Brooklyn, too, so I guess the only thing that's eliminated is New Jersey."

"I hear that some of those towns have become go-to."

"Except that I grew up there and I know the pluses and minuses for Short Hills, Montclair, Maplewood."

They were nearing a complex of cottages as the dog began wagging its tail furiously.

"Marlon!" someone called, and Marlon sprinted to dwelling 6 and the loving embrace of a woman wearing a black swimsuit, along with a bandana around her head. She quickly transferred the paisley kerchief to Marlon's neck as he smiled and licked upward.

"Hi, I'm Jeanie, part of Marlon's team. Yes, he is named for Brando—not the fish," she said, smiling widely. "We would have named a girl Brandy."

"I studied some of his films in a class," said Grant. "He wasn't always that nice to women."

"I was asked to watch his technique in method acting. That early Brando wasn't exactly hard on the eyes," added Marissa.

"What a coincidence," said Jeanie. "I was thinking of starting a theater group here. Well, not here exactly. We take Marlon here so that he can run after traps and splash into whoever he encounters on the beach. Today it was you. Actually, we live part of the year in Eastham; it's two towns over."

"Sam's," said Grant.

"The best," said Jeanie.

"Um, could someone fill me in?" asked Marissa. Marlon began to lick her knees, then suddenly leapt to reach her face with slurps. "I'm the theater person, the actress."

"Really?" said Jeanie. She looked Marissa up and down. "This is not surprising," she added.

Marissa blushed as Grant came to her defense. "She's not just another pretty face," he said, and Jeanie nodded. "She's as talented as any actor her age I've seen. And, by the way, Sam's has the best chocolate cookies on the Cape. An exceptional go-to deli."

"So sweet is my boyfriend," said Marissa.

"We're meeting tonight, hoping for six of us, to actually start this theater. Why not come along?" asked Jeanie. "Both of you. I can tell you"—she looked at Grant—"know something about the arts, too, yes?"

"Yes," he said. "I mean, about performing arts. I've been on the other side, at least when it comes to independent films, on camera, directing, and I love designing sets."

"You look like the director type," said Jeanie. "I mean that as a compliment. Come in the house for a minute?" she asked. The dog began to leap and twirl, then settled on licking Grant's long fingers.

"I went to acting classes when I was a kid and did a number of plays, but I've always been more comfortable on the other side. What about you?" he asked Jeanie.

"Well. Where to begin—or maybe that's too, too much. My family vacationed here, or near here, in Harwichport. My summer memories from childhood involve kids theater: *The Wizard of Oz*, *Alice*, *Sleeping Beauty*. Then I graduated, so to speak, to *Peter Pan* and *The Sound of Music*. Stop."

"Stop?" asked Marissa.

"I notice when I'm doing all of the talking and, worse, it's about me," said Jeanie. "I take over too often. The new theater will be collaborative."

"Hey, we were just out for a walk to see the bay, this town. I mean, I don't really know much about it, but Grant does."

"As does Mac, my friend." She paused. "We've been thinking about creating this theater thing for months. Join us later?" She pointed to a rounded porch. "On the deck at 7:00. Yes, we are gathering here in P-town to talk about a place in Eastham."

Grant looked at Marissa, who nodded. "That would be cool," he said. "I mean, making theater."

***

"Mac, these are the friends I met earlier today: Grant and Marita?"

"Marissa," said Marissa, thinking that Marita sounded whorish and resenting herself for going there. "Everyone messes up my name," she said. "I guess it's not as bad as the names kids get these days. Mine would be Amarissa or something like that."

"I'm not really Mac. It was shortened from Mac-Gregor, which is a family name. Actually, my name is Henry."

"No way," said Grant, who added, "I should talk since my actual name is Grantland."

"That leaves me, Jeanie. That's my real, actual name, and I've always felt that it sounds like a baby name. I mean, really, it's 'Jeanie this' and 'Jeanie that.' It sounds like I'm a doll or something."

Just then, Marlon, the irresistible black Lab, hurtled into the room, tail flying and tongue wagging.

"Chill," said Jeanie, and the dog sat on her foot. "He wants to act in whatever we come up with."

"There aren't that many roles for dogs," said Marissa. "*Annie*? *Peter Pan*? Anybody have others?"

Mac looked around, then upward, and he seemed to be air sculpting, configuring a plan or creating brushstrokes for a phantom painting. It was quickly silent. Grant looked at Marissa, whose eyes fleetingly raised, but she lowered her gaze before anyone else could see.

A whoosh of wind smacked open an idle screen door.

"We want to start a theater. That's the goal. I produce, and Jeanie designs everything: sets, costumes, and tech, too, if need be—lights and sound."

"I want to be on stage," said Marissa. "Now or soon enough. Where do you fit in, Grant?"

"Promote it, build it. Help Jeanie create. I don't want to act," said Grant. "When do we begin?"

"Who directs?" asked Marissa.

"Well, I have," said Mac. "I could. Do I want to?"

"I think we have to figure out what play we're going to do first, and then maybe it will become clear," said Jeanie. Just then, Marlon barked four times in succession as though he agreed.

All laughed as Jeanie continued, "He's not only hoping he isn't left on the beach but also that starring isn't out of the question."

With that, something crashed—ka-boom!—above them. Mac jumped up, trailed by Grant, to track the explosion. The two of them ran around the house and looked up to the sky but saw nothing. They returned, smiling at one another as if sharing a secret.

"A large branch smacked down," said Mac. "Some great designer in the sky trying to trick us."

"Get real, Mac," said Jeanie, "instead of working your stuff on people who don't know what you're like."

"No trees then?" asked Marissa. "You're making it up?"

"Just think of it as a set device. Someone just dropped a clunky, clanking wooden hunk above you. What do you do?"

"Scream!" shrieked Marissa.

On a two-second delay, everyone erupted into laughter.

"Woe to the woman who needs a knock on the head to fully live!" Marissa said. "This is not in my contract. Ow!"

"Let's play with that," said Jeanie. "What would you do, Grant, if a giant bird landed with a smack on your long, wavy locks."

"Brush it off, scold it, and then advise it never to return," he said. "Unless the winged one dropped a load, too. Then I would be forced to react, to return the favor."

"Meaning?"

"Who needs bird crap?" Grant answered.

Mac interrupted. "Do you—or does anyone—really think couples who just met can start a theater? The swimming upstream thing for sure but we are about to push forward on this."

"We are totally good new friends," said Jeanie, "so we haven't any old incidents, difficulties, or relationships to stall this. Besides, we have Marlon!"

"Yo, Marlon!" said Grant. "He will lead us to the theater."

The next day, the new friends reconvened. Jeanie had reserved space for them at the Unitarian fellowship site in Eastham. She and Mac, months before, had gone to an open mic there, and Jeanie had stepped up to sing an Alison Krauss favorite of hers. Soon after, they started attending Sunday morning services there on an irregular basis. Organized and led by those in the community rather than by a member of the clergy, these occasions could be either winning or boring. One never knew. Jeanie and Mac liked the spirit and warmth of the place and, upon occasion, it was both heartening and exhilarating to be there. Additionally, the site was easy about sharing space. Thus, Jeanie brought the contingent there the next day for a brown-bag lunch to be followed by theater discussion.

"This is it," she said as Marlon, also attending, barked loudly three times before Mac shushed him. "It's not like a formal sanctuary, and I guess this area in the front, slightly elevated, could be a stage. It is not typically warm in here even during midsummer. Shouldn't it be?"

"I brought a script I've been working on," said Marissa. "I realize we don't know one another, but, well, could we dive into something? Would you mind?"

"I'm in," said Mac. "I will make whatever you want."

"Actually, this is a one-act play I've written. We can do this together. At least, I think so."

"Okay," said Jeanie. "I mean, why not?'

"I just want everyone here to know that I haven't heard a word of it, and I've never seen any portion of it—for what it's worth," said Grant. "When have you been working on it, Marissa?"

"It's all on my tablet," Marissa replied. "So every time I've opened it up, I've gone to the script, which I labeled Script. I guess we need copies. Didn't think of that. Can't work on it without hard copies."

Mac jumped in. "We have two iPads and a laptop. Should be able to transfer it over without too much trouble, no? Let's do it."

Jeanie, taking the cue, was already out the door, calling over her shoulder, "I'll be back in less than fifteen minutes with the devices!"

That left time for the remaining three people to get better acquainted.

"Jeanie and Marlon ran into you guys on the beach?" asked Mac.

"Something like that," said Marissa. "The dog was the connector."

"Not at all surprising to me. Marlon goes everywhere with us, and we sort of inherited him," said Mac. "He doesn't want to lose us, and we are desperate to include him, well, pretty much all the time."

"It sounds like there's a story behind all of this, so do tell," said Grant.

"Well, Jeanie and I met a couple of summers ago. My family has been coming to the Cape forever, and she was working in a clothing store in Chatham. You want more?"

"Are you kidding?" asked Marissa. "This is where I start to listen. Always a romance girl, that's me."

"You are from . . .?" asked Mac.

"New Jersey. I know—the most unromantic place ever, but you might be surprised," she answered.

"It's okay," said Mac. "I'm from Rockland County."

"Close enough to the Hudson and not all that far from Palisades," said Grant. "Know it well. I grew up less than half an hour away. Marissa's in Brooklyn just now, that's where she lives"

"Not shocking, really," said Mac. "I bet you're like me and did some theater when you were a kid."

"The stage intimidated me but I was in one show," Grant said. "I tried doing some music, which was a better fit. That and creating scenic effects. My first band experience was with *Fame* and then some other gigs. I still think of myself as more musician and tech guy than actor.

What do you play?"

"I would have said drums a couple of years ago, guitar last year, but now I am a keyboard player. It all relates, but I can compose best on piano. Writing."

"In a slightly different mode, me, too," said Grant. "I write nonfiction, and Marissa, who still acts, is starting to write plays. Pretty serious stuff."

Jeanie burst through the screen door, carrying laptops pressed to her shirt. "Okay, anyone who knows what to do, step up. We need to make Marissa's work accessible."

"Okay, just give me a few minutes to give you a sense of this somewhat biographical script," said Marissa. "It's about this girl and boy in the Southwest. Sweet story just developing. She's an actress, or at least she has always wanted that. He's more on the craft side of the arts. They both like to hike, and they're in Moab. What could be better?"

"This is good so far," said Jeannie.

"I like it, too," added Mac.

"Let's call the main character Mary Ann. In supporting roles are her sister, Carolee, and Carolee's boyfriend, JJ. I was thinking you two could be the leads, and if Grant doesn't mind, he and I would take the supporting characters."

"As a non-performer, that sounds like a perfect fit," said Grant. "Fewer lines for me to say and mess up," he laughed.

"I could, on the other hand, turn all of this into a once-upon-a-time fairy tale," said Marissa.

"Go for it," said Jeanie.

"Look through an arch and Shangri-La, paradise on the other side," said Marissa. "That is in the original, but the rest isn't. I'm making this up; it's not part of the script." Marissa looked around the room to see if she had everyone's attention. "It's 110 degrees in mid-August. As a girl from the East, she cannot say whether this is dry heat or what might be the suitable caption for this picture. Her sense of smell, though, is heightened and she really can't explain it."

"Go on," said Mac. "This is great."

"Something about my mantra. I think that is what comes next?"

Grant interrupted. "Marissa, isn't that part from the Berkshires?"

"No, let's stay with Moab, with the romance," she said. "Besides, and I don't know why I haven't told you, my parents are coming to Moab. Trying to unify our family." She paused. "It's been a long while."

Chapter 6

Moab

May 2011

MARISSA KNEW THAT SHE needed a more specific sense of the terrain before her play would resonate with anyone on or off stage. *Too familiar for its own good*, she thought. She kept thinking about her sister. Marissa and Grant had left town literally overnight. Marissa had essentially run out on Diana, to whom she owed something more than a lame explanation. It had now been quite a while and, if they went back now, Marissa might be able to mend the wound. She knew it was her doing.

That was not the only reason Marissa wanted to return, and she knew it: She also wanted Grant there (recalling a moment on a large, smooth rock) —and then they would fall asleep with his arm across her chest and belly. That was the missing photo, and she was in pursuit of the full movie version. Marissa would never say so, but it was fine to think it, imagine it, dream about it. He was a sweet guy, and he was supportive of her. He allowed—even encouraged—both the wondrous

Berkshire chapter and the short Cape Cod episode to happen.

That short time with Diana was troubling to Marissa. Diana's boyfriend was driving her crazy, and Marissa had tried to be sympathetic but didn't understand what all the fuss was about. Her sister was ballistic about the guy gaining some weight. So what? That was then.

⚜ ⚜

Marissa hadn't remembered the lighting in Moab: the shadows, the late-day mix of bright and softer hues. Sitting by the quesadilla truck, she looked behind her and saw what seemed to be four shades of red. She thought about all the different colors, like magenta and rose, in a box of Crayola crayons. She looked across the street at the ice cream store which had been there for years and realized she wanted a large sundae with whipped cream, hot fudge, and a cherry on top. It was fun enough to fantasize about, but she resisted the impulse.

Grant came strolling across the street, coffee in hand.

"Where to and when?" he asked.

"No place mentioned in any book or guide or tourist advisory," she said. "Let's drive out some-where and stop and walk. Okay?"

"Is this is part of your play, Marissa?"

She held his hand. "Someday, maybe," she said. "Truth be told, one of my reasons for coming back out here was to gather specifics and material to develop the script. If I ever do complete it, yes, I'll need those details. Otherwise, you know, it will sound like I'm making up the whole thing. I was writing that part on lasting impressions ." After a pause, she added, "Also, though, there's the script of life."

"Let my guess: your sister?"

"We did kind of leave without notice," said Marissa. "I was thinking maybe we could meet her or them at Eklectica, if she's even still with that guy. You know—the hippie restaurant."

"Sure. Especially if I can embarrass you in front of a brunch crowd," said Grant.

"Try me," said Marissa, lunging at Grant. "Meanwhile, I want an ice cream cone," she said, dragging him across the street. "Then, let's drive to Canyonlands. I've never been there."

Grant said, "I was there, once, briefly. Never at this hour, though. More like late in the afternoon. I heard that the park is something else at night. Let's bring some food, eat, and then explore. What say you?"

"Maybe that'll have the feel of a movie. As a performer, I'm in. Why not?"

"I just have one other and maybe connected thought," said Grant. "Would your sister and her friend meet up with us? Would she do that? 'Two more on this expedition,' as someone once said in *Pooh*?"

Marissa tugged at a clip and allowed her thick hair to tumble forward. She started laughing. "You surprise me. Sure, I will ask Diana and maybe she will bring LG. Let me call her right away." She walked a few paces away from Grant and did just that. "Diana says maybe she can get LG and get together with us at Island in the Sky in a few hours. We should start driving now and see what happens, yes?"

As they drove, Marissa contrasted, in her mind, every shade of tan, brown, and red with the greens of the Berkshire hills. The latter was familiar and comforting; this brought up feelings of adventure and challenge. Not that she was about to hike straight up in the dark or anything like that. If she tried to, she might be required to grab a rope or mount two or three ladders in two or three minutes. All the advisories, too, warned that hikers needed to carry plenty of water and, if need be, a hearty snack. No food to buy on the premises. She knew they would be 6,000 feet up, and it sounded astonishing to her. She also wondered if all of this was a likely second act, the first beginning with "Boys and girls meet at Delicate Arch." That sounded like a lyric.

She needed for something to happen in her play. Not a fan of zombies or disasters, she started spinning possible scenarios in her mind: someone falls off a cliff or a blazing fire breaks out or there's an attack by an animal. No, no, and no.

What, however, if someone, during a relationship crisis, ran off—and those in pursuit could not locate them. High melodrama, sure. Could it happen? Not exactly, but that scenario, if temporary, might yield to something real.

"Stop there!" she suddenly shouted at Grant.

He slammed on the brakes. They left the car and walked a bit on a nearby trail.

"Look up," she said, and he did. "It looks like a person carrying a dog on her back," said Marissa.

"We have to get up there. Do something."

"Come on," Grant said.

Without letting go of her hand, he pulled her quickly up a short trail. When they reached the top, they discovered two people in their mid-twenties, arguing. On her back, the woman carried a dog that was wedged into a carrier more typically used to carry a child. The dog was tiny but surprisingly calm as if it was used to this procedure. The young woman held the hand of a blonde-headed toddler. Perched atop a hill twenty-five yards away from the disconcerting scene below them, Grant and Marissa paused. They heard a rendition of "Here Comes the Sun" emanating sweetly from a device and walked toward the couple with the bouncy baby child and the dog.

"Do you want help? Need anything?" called Grant.

"You don't happen to have any dog biscuits, do you?" asked the man. "He likes them, but we forgot to pack some and now he has a mental clock that is saying it's time for a snack."

"No, sorry," said Grant. "From a distance, it looked like maybe something was wrong."

"We have an old-fashioned CD player, and it keeps playing The Beatles over and over," said the young woman. "So we're caught between no song or the same song again and again and again."

"Yes, but what about your baby?" asked Marissa.

The young man, smoothing the child's hair, said, "She's happy to be here. We read that there is an amazing purplish, deep-blue sculpted cat—a panther maybe—that someone created up further. It's in a ways, and we just thought to hike."

"Really? At the top of a steep hill someone sculpted it?" Grant asked.

The young woman replied, "We're both artists, and we believe it's possible."

"Let's go," said Marissa. "Which way?"

"Is it soft or a stone?" asked Grant.

"I'm not sure, but we're hoping it could amuse Lily," said the young woman. "I'm Sadie, by the way.

I'm glad you want to go with us, even though I haven't any idea why you climbed up this hill—other than, maybe, you're Beatles fans?"

"Marissa thought something was wrong. She saw you from a distance," said Grant.

Sadie started to laugh. "I'm not laughing at you," she said quickly. "We don't exactly match the model presented in a child-rearing book, do we? Look at us: the baby, Scooch the dog, me, Markus, and one song that keeps playing over and over till we shut it off."

"Same with us," said Marissa. "Grant and I met at a bar in Moab. It was like we were under a spell. The coming together, then to the Berkshires, Provincetown, and now back here. It's as though there's a force coming from the rocks"—she gazed upward—"and I think there must be an arch out there somewhere."

"Yes," Markus said. "We want to make it to a specific but not-often-visited arch and a sculpture."

"It's one not listed in the usual guidebooks, I assume," said Marissa.

Grant asked, "Why is it special?"

"Well," said Sadie, "it's named Genie, supposedly for a rock configuration that looks like Aladdin's lamp, according to this old paperback we found in a tiny Moab bookstore."

"Seriously," said Marissa, "I didn't mean it that way. It could be real. That's the kind of device used in certain types of theater. The people who are too literal, they don't get it. Why not?"

Suddenly, "Here Comes the Sun," which had faded away, began to play once again, as Markus, on pitch, sang along. Marissa, having done musicals right through college, easily harmonized.

"Come with us," said Sadie, her hand intertwined with the child's. "It will be a fun walk, and what have you got to lose?" She motioned to a trail leading upward.

"You up for this, Marissa? My take is why not?" Grant said.

"The only thing is, we're guessing on the path. I sorta think the arch is over there; we know that much. But it isn't like people hike there every day."

They wound tightly around a rim, and Marissa couldn't help but look downward and shudder. She thought about her sister and that boyfriend of hers. Something fuzzy was touching her, and she realized it could not possibly be Grant, whose hands were fairly smooth. She looked down and there was

Scooch, the dog, nuzzling her. She saw that Grant was smiling, even laughing, at her.

"All theater, wouldn't you say, my dear?" he asked.

Just then, she slipped—but not badly—and happened to see an etching carved into a rock formation that otherwise was out of view. It was a lamp with a spout pointing slightly left of center from the route they'd taken.

"This way," said Marissa. "Follow me. It's the lamp directing us," she added and motioned to the rock.

Scooch caught on immediately, encouraging everyone else as he pulled forward. Sadie was carrying Lily, and they followed the dog. Markus was next, and Grant called from behind, "I'll bring up the rear." Together, they formed an unlikely caterpillar-like train. Marissa had to hold herself back so that everyone was in sync.

Lily raised her eyebrows toward Markus. As if conducting an orchestra, he lifted his arm and together they began singing actual lyrics and then making up more for "You Are My Sunshine." "Here Comes the Sun" had run its course.

The gleaming light, early platinum, caused Marissa to stop short. She threw both of her hands over her eyes, which suddenly watered. She saw an image that resembled a lamp, but it hovered beyond the morning sun's rays. Marissa shook her head and hair, then squinted to focus. It wasn't really a lamp but seemingly a pen-and-ink sketch someone had drawn.

"Look!" She shouted to the others.

No one, however, reacted. Marissa waved upward and beyond, but knew that she was alone in the experience. She gathered herself and marched forward. The dog, Scooch, scrambled free and ran to the formation. Marissa raced just behind. She traced the lines of the lamp with her hands. Scooch glanced around and seemed poised to mark the spot.

Suddenly, though, the dog lost its balance and, too close to the edge, fell forward and off the tiny cliff. Sadie's frightened scream reached the dog's ears almost instantly, and Scooch immediately shot out his paws and landed, fairly softly, on a trail below.

Everyone cheered as Marissa said, "I got it! The denouement! Sorry about the fancy word. I mean I've figured out the ending, the fitting conclusion to all of this: Grant and me; my question with my sister, and a moment, right now, when I can fly." With that, before anyone could stop her, Marissa ran to the point where the path and the ridge converged. "It looks like someone's drawn a rainbow river," she said. "Look."

Grant protectively leaned across. "Astonishing," he said. "It's out here, and it looks like a Rothko."

"You're in O'Keeffe country," said Markus. "But I know what you mean. It's nearly fire engine red, too."

"Seems impossible," said Sadie. "A wine shade—and almost always hues of brown, tan, olive green."

Before they could react, Scooch, catching scent of something, took off again, this time dropping down a dozen feet to a landing. The dog looked back at them and smiled.

The baby, wiggling within her mother's firm hold, spotted the dog and waved toward the panorama.

Grant said, "Maybe this is the key moment of this movie, the one including Marissa and me, the one that began around here, went to the Berkshires, now back to this spot. Look out there, M. It's so cinematic and so surreal. Maybe it's telling us something. It makes me feel like 'Forever Young,' which I only recently learned Bob Dylan wrote and sang first. I mean, it's us and the baby and the dog and these people. This vision before us, what does it all mean?"

With that, as if someone had dropped a bucket full of lukewarm water directly on them, it began raining. Sadie and Markus danced as she held the baby aloft and he tickled Scooch.

"Lily, say Scooch," her mother suggested.

"Sooch," Lily said.

"With a C," said Markus as he mouthed and demonstrated.

"Cooch!" cried Lily.

Everyone followed the dog, who had paused to carefully peer into an alcove. Grant moved to lead and heard a voice as they approached the opening which, he thought, might be a cave. He bent to see more carefully, then jerked his head around and called, "Marissa, someone you know is peacefully singing in here."

"Sure," she said.

"Your sister, wearing a Jersey Shore hoodie and playing guitar," said Grant, as Marissa approached and leaned over. "I'm not kidding."

"Dee, what are you doing in there?"

"Singing Joni Mitchell songs. I wasn't old enough to hear these, but my sister, a true flower child actor, taught them to me," she said and laughed.

"You're sitting in half a cave, playing folk songs and acting as though this is perfectly normal."

"It's beautiful in here, Issa. Sit down."

While coiling herself into the opening, Marissa wondered about Diana's boyfriend and asked, "Where's your guy?"

"Probably out drinking. That's what he does," said Diana.

"No wonder you're keeping your distance from him. But here, Dee?"

"I was certain he wouldn't track me this far, Marissa. The usual arches, he knows. Lately I admitted to myself that I didn't want anything more to do with him—and now he wants me." She put down the guitar and replaced it, in her hand, with a ceramic detail sculpting tool. She carved, on the cave wall, an etching of a dog. Marissa, improvising, used a tissue to add bright white, giving it a Day-Glo effect.

"That's amazing, Dee," said Marissa.

"What's amazing? I haven't seen you in a few months and it hasn't been that easy a period. I've been taking care of a friend's dog which is not white, but it is a Lab and the shape is sort of like what you see here. I've been line drawing. I did that back in high school. The painting part is new, and I have to thank you for that touch. What about you?"

"You remember Grant?"

"I do. Sorry that when I met you, I was right in the middle of the mostly hate but part love thing with LG."

Just then, baby Lily began to chirp, talk, sing—but only she knew what the sounds meant. It was a delightful language including bits and pieces of actual words. Marissa windmilled one of her arms slowly, asking everyone to step forward to meet her sister. A huge, darkening cloud seemed to descend upon them, sending, directly downward, a steady stream of water.

"Get in! Everyone in here!" Marissa said as she motioned to Sadie, Markus, the baby, and Scooch, too. Pressing up against one another, all of them jammed into the alcove. Marissa continued, "This is my sister, Diana. Diana, you know my boyfriend, Grant, and these are our new friends." Scooch, on cue, scampered from one person to the next.

Diana smiled widely and warmly as Marissa realized she had not often seen her sister at rest and at peace with herself. But it seemed as though Diana had found these things here, of all places, within the confines of a cave. Claps of thunder echoed, suddenly, above. The dog twitched, and the baby began to cry.

"Huddle up," said Markus, and everyone pressed closer.

"It's never a good idea to mess with lightning," Grant said.

A moment later, a flashing silver bolt zapped at them, striking the CD player in the midst of Paul McCartney singing "I'll Follow the Sun." The device had finally allowed for a new tune. Shards of plastic went flying in several directions, sparing the cave dwellers—almost. Scooch's tail, protruding slightly outside the alcove, intercepted the lightning. The dog yelped in pain but escaped without critical injury. Instantly, the lightning bounced at Grant who simultaneously covered his face and ducked away.

Marissa and Sadie, together, hugged and comforted the dog, seemingly aware that he had not been severely wounded but shocked just the same by the lightning. Lily held to Markus, who comforted the child with one hand while stroking Sadie's flowing locks with the other. Grant placed his hands on Diana's shoulders and began to massage them.

"Not used to this," she said, relaxing to the rhythm of his fingers. She began to sway as both Marissa and Sadie sat silently. Markus ambled over, picked up Scooch, and pointed him skyward. "Seek the sun, little dog. Bring us peace," he said, whereupon Scooch seemingly grinned.

Marissa said, "Sing with me this reprise version of 'You Are My Sunshine.'"

Part III

Chapter 7

Harry and Carolyn Southwest Redux

June 2011

HARRY WHISTLED LENNON AND McCartney's "Come Together."

Carolyn softly added, "over me."

They were deplaning in Vegas during the early evening hours, but what were they thinking? About their children and what this reunion would bring after all these years? About the rental car and how long till they reached Moab? From what they recalled, it would take more than six hours, but Harry moved along. Perhaps it would take them five-plus. They could always stay on the Strip overnight or go directly to the house. But if they chose a night at a motel, for whatever reason, they should tell Diana or Marissa.

Harry and Carolyn had married just over four decades earlier. Long ago, they had come to understand each other's gestures and idiosyncrasies. Thus, when Carolyn stood and looked at the sky,

Harry knew they would be driving across the desert.

Harry Reflects: 1

Was it really 1970 when I sweated my way through a few weeks, on and off, taking census when my heart and body pined for Carolyn? Cambridge is now a blur: I spent four or five days there in that living room on the sofa, which had bedsprings popping up all over. Press one down, and the spring next to it stabbed you. I had wanted Carolyn for years but was able to admit to myself, finally, that I was too afraid to pursue her. That guy Edison pushed me to follow my instincts. The trajectory: Lower East Side, Boston, Moab.

We were out of our minds to get married—just two kids who took turns being infatuated with one another. What an understatement! Compared to me, Carolyn was sane. She had gone to Boston to get some perspective. On the other hand, when she came to see me in Cambridge, she snuggled up and climbed on me almost before saying hello.

Next thing you know, we're back on Houston Street. The group. Community meals. Uncle and aunt figures who are watchful, hoping we glide rather than trip through early adulthood. We're both from The Island, and we don't want to go back. What happens? We choose a fancy suburban town in Jersey and find a house to rent. After all, we couldn't pretend to be urban dwellers, having grown up in bedroom community towns.

I got a job as a receptionist at a jazz club in Montclair. Before I knew it, I was managing the joint. Carolyn had already been certified to teach high school. She scored a job teaching reading to tough kids but, soon enough, became a full-time member of the English Department. The women's movement was flourishing, and she had the green light to celebrate feminist politicos and writers like Gloria Steinem, Doris Lessing, Adrienne Rich, and Bella Abzug.

Our parents were neither thrilled nor put off by our decision to marry. We might have been young, impulsive, and even stupid, but we were good-hearted and we were working and thinking. By the time we were in our early thirties.,
I began to push for kids. People would ask me if I planned to manage the club forever and, if not, what did I really want to be? When I would say a great father, they would raise eyebrows, shrug shoulders, maybe smile. The 70s were supposedly a liberated time when gender roles weren't so rigid. Still, if you were a man who could not formulate a direct and impressive career path, well, people doubted you.

Carolyn was either sharper or more mature or both. She kept insisting that it was still early, that we could wait till our mid-thirties for children. She was right, but I was primed.

It seemed, in a flash, that we had a baby. I know that's easy for me, the male, to say. Little Marissa took after her mother: precocious and magnetic. Her hair was immediately dark and full. She hit all of the milestones early: walking, talking, bike riding.

She was a childhood orator and conversationalist. We called her president-in-training and imagined her having a career in politics.

We doted on her as if she were a special princess. We considered that she might be our only daughter, and Carolyn and I agreed that would be fine.

Several years later,, Diana was born. She was some squirmer right from the start. A happy baby, though, as was Marissa. The older one was completely thrilled to have a little sister whom she could boss around. They played together well. We didn't have enough money to buy the very latest playground set for the backyard, but I was pretty good at cobbling together a knockoff. The girls were delighted to jump aboard whatever we had. Generous grandparents spared no dime when it came to the little ones, so our house was filled with games and gizmos galore, as well as puzzles featuring Cinderella, Sleeping Beauty, Snow White, Aladdin—you name it.

At one point, Marissa asked us if we liked girls better than boys. When we wondered why she thought so, Marissa said, "Well, me and Diana are girls and, in school, the girls are smarter."

Carolyn and I managed to be fiscally stable since she did some lawyering in the house before her school guidance work. I filled in the dead spots by writing articles for the daily newspaper in Montclair. And the graphic design biz, too. I didn't make a whole lot of money, but, we successfully cobbled together income. My gig at the jazz club added just enough. Remember that this was, by now, it must have been into the 1980s, Carolyn was encouraged, pushed to keep teaching a "Women in Literature" course she designed. She was professionally happy, and she brought in a helpful paycheck.

Until Marissa was pre-adolescent, we really did not have any major issues raising our daughters. Sure, they could bicker upon occasion, but so what? They were sisters who would bond together if anyone even glanced sideways at one or the other. Marissa and Diana were protective of each other. Physically, I mean in terms of their bodies, the girls had little in common.

Marissa, with a flair for the dramatic, developed early. While this drew too much unwanted attention from boys, her look, she realized, might be a match for some acting roles in school plays. Diana was slender, even wiry, and from the beginning a girl who could run, jump, and scale with the best of them. Thankfully, they were not competitive and rivalry wasn't an issue. Each became the other's cheerleader.

Marissa couldn't wait to be in a play. When she was in sixth grade and Kid Theater was doing *Peter Pan*, she desperately wanted to be Tiger Lily. She ended up getting cast as Captain Hook. The director told Marissa she could pull off the bad guy role better than anyone else since very few boys wanted anything to do with onstage parts. When the show finally opened and Marissa appeared beneath a frizzed-out black wig, a claw for her hand, Diana was shocked. But her big sister had developed a growl of a voice, and, with blackened eyeshadow, she was a hoot and a half. Marissa stole the show, and Diana yelped with joy. Siblings!

Diana was a blindingly fast sprinter, beating many boys when they raced just for fun. During inter-school track meets, Marissa sang "Go, Dee! Go, Dee!" as her little sister snagged one victory after another. She represented the school in county track meets and took home a number of trophies.

A greater issue was this: Their worlds were separate ones, and while their bedrooms were adjacent, their perceptions were sometimes dissimilar. Marissa wondered how anyone could assign top priority to racing faster than anyone else. Diana could not understand her big sister's zeal to constantly become someone else. Perhaps the deeper question was whether either of them was comfortable within her own skin.

And then there were the boyfriends.

Marissa constantly dodged teen boys who wished to brush up against her, take her to the movies, walk her home from school. She tried wearing clothing that concealed her figure, but adolescent guys couldn't resist fantasizing about her. In addition to her sexual allure, she was also both strong of will and stature. She liked the attention but pushed young men aside if they grabbed her—until Adam, a fellow high school actor who was slight but smart. At first good friends, they became a couple during their junior year when they appeared together in *Our Town*. But by the time they graduated, Marissa and Adam were no more. When I asked her what went wrong, she smiled and said, "It was great until it wasn't"—a phrase that has stayed with me to this day.

Boys whose eyes went straight to girls' chests weren't immediately taken with Diana. Watching her older sister's suitors march to the front door of the house, Diana wished that just one time the wanna-be-dating call would be for her. She didn't expect a boy two grades behind her to seek her out. Riley, though, saw his mirror image in Diana. He, too, was thin. He did not run track, but he was a speedy lead-off hitter on the baseball team. Whenever he was on base, he was a threat to steal. Eventually, Diana came to terms with the fact that, while he was a couple of years younger, he was sweet and she loved watching him play ball. They agreed, however, when Diana was about to leave for college, to hit the pause button. She was soon gone; he was not forgotten, but it was never the same.

It is possible that each was jealous of the other, but that's only my theory. I was a lucky father: My daughters did love me, and ever so often, each told me so. For me, it was always family before workplace. It never occurred to me that paying too much attention to my children could feel, to them, like a combination of pressure and suffocation. Is it too late to apologize?

Somehow, probably because Carolyn maintained some perspective, Marissa, first, and then Diana flew away from the nest relatively intact. The older one, predictably, went to NYU to study acting, back when it was somewhat possible to get in. The training was rigorous, highly structured, and included multiple opportunities to perform in everything: classics, modern plays, and musicals.

Diana found Hampshire College to be a neat fit. The indoor gym had a rock-climbing wall, kids were encouraged to kayak, and she was able to formulate her own program. She balanced various liberal arts courses with outdoor activities and ended up focusing on freedom and hiking. Her final project included a photographic essay with pictures she took and interviews she conducted with everyone from Olympic sprinters to mountain climbers. Impressive.

After Diana left home, Carolyn and I looked at each other, acknowledging that we had only us now. While other parents had struggled during their children's rebellious adolescence, we did well navigating that block of time. Perhaps, however, our devotion to the girls came at our expense as a loving couple. For a time, we danced around but not with each other. Carolyn's reputation as being caring, nurturing, thoughtful, and direct meant that more than one school sought her to problem solve. I shifted to full time at the newspaper and soon became an arts editor. I retained the jazz club gig part time. The balance was fulfilling but, I now see, left little time for Carolyn, who was, herself, a workaholic.

Our children had left home when Carolyn and I began to lose touch with each other emotionally. We didn't yell or scream, and there wasn't a build-to-a-slow-boil scenario. Instead, we each retreated. Rather than growing furious with Carolyn or myself, I became numb. She was always self-aware and, in conjunction with her listening skills, realized we were separating. We did not live apart, but we were not together. We slept in the same bed, but each of us stayed on our own side. We went long stretches without talking until one day Carolyn said, "Remember the heat we generated in 1970 just by being in the same room?"

I said something like, "Yes, before my heart attack."

"It was mild, Harry. Just beyond a scare," she responded.

"The exact words were, 'The heart muscle is damaged, and we think not severely but no one knows.' That's what sent me over the edge or the ledge or whatever that phrase is," I said.

"They also said you could gradually resume, within reason, pretty much all normal activities," she said.

Some people respond to a serious medical situation with fervor and the will to fight through. I am not one of those individuals. In my eyes, I was now damaged goods: old, ruined, washed-up, and a loser. I let Carolyn in on a small portion of the self-assessment, and she tried her best to provide reason, insight, and encouragement. I listened, but her wise perspective eluded me. I dug myself into a deeper hole, wondering just when a major and more massive attack would level me forever. I considered this a given.

I retreated into myself and, convinced that my sexuality was permanently limited, backed away from Carolyn. She sympathized and reassured me that she understood. Patience was her virtue, not mine. To this day, I do not believe she found someone else. Still, she needed camaraderie and sought this with colleagues because I no longer met her emotional needs.

We coexisted and were not enemies, but those were the years we were the most distant from each other. Eventually, something had to give. You could cut the tension within our two-person home with a knife. Carolyn and I realized we were tiptoeing around an abyss. We needed to do something together, and, because of my reticence, it would not be sexual. We decided to try singing together as we had during our brief chapter in the East Village. Decades later, she had retained her voice but mine had dropped an octave and lost clarity. I considered this part of a gradual, accumulating decline

I started drinking at the club. Jazz and alcohol, back then, and maybe many others, comingled. All I had to do was tell Carolyn that the job was keeping me later; she never questioned that. I was at the front desk and began to hang with the performers after a gig. I came home obviously drunk more than once. The first time, she bought my story that a drink or two turned into four. The pattern, however, continued, and I fed and fueled it. The problem was that I liked drinking.

Carolyn was not pleased but, as a skilled therapist, chose not to confront me. She responded by creating, for herself, a life away from home. It wasn't surprising that her workplace became a primary rather than a secondary social outlet. Whereas Carolyn shied away from collegial get-togethers during her years as an active mom to Marissa and Diana, she now became a joiner and a participant.

Okay, she had a boyfriend and I had a girl-friend—though neither of us slept with them or anyone else. Our own sexual relationship, how-ever, was on ice. It was icy. It was nonexistent.

I tried a variety of instruments when I was still in elementary school. For a time, I could really sing. I imagine myself as a keyboard man in a soft rock 'n' roll band. One of the women in a group at the jazz club, a band called The Four Shades because they wore sunglasses, told me she could teach me beginning elements of piano training. Before I knew it, she and I were hanging out after gigs. She would sit me at the piano, then lean on me as she placed my hands on the keyboard. I felt an electric charge riffle through my body the first time she did that.

Carolyn had a lovely, wide-ranging voice. She had grown up accompanying herself on guitar as she learned folk songs. She sang in chorus both through high school and college. It was natur-al when a longtime choir director at her school retired that Carolyn quickly stepped into that role. She became close to the kids, especially a boy with a deep baritone and a dark beard. She worked with him on breathing exercises that might allow him to reach into a higher octave. She sang with him and chose "So in Love" from *Kiss Me Kate* as a piece they could do together.

Our schedules were such that we spent little time together at the house. I would go to the paper in the late morning, then, some days, to the club before or after the dinner hour. Carolyn left for school at 7:30 and would return at 4:00 or so. That changed when she took on the choir, which rehearsed during the late afternoons.

One day, everything imploded—albeit in slow motion. I had finished up at the paper and stopped at home for an early light dinner before heading back out for the club. Carolyn was in the living room with a young man. We had an upright piano. He was at the bench as she hovered behind him. I heard her, as I was opening the front door, say, "In through your nose, Randy, and out through your mouth."

Carolyn was surprised to see me but recovered quickly and said, "Oh, Harry, this is Randy. I've told you all about him."

I recall consciously shrugging my shoulders as if this was news to me.

She went on: "I've been coaching him on his voice. You know that's something I really like to do." She lifted her hand off his shoulder and placed it at her side. I knew.

"He needs a ride back to the school," she said. It was around five in the afternoon, but I simply said, "Fine with me."

I made myself a sandwich, put it in a bag, grabbed a can of seltzer, and went off to the club. After the gig that night, I drove home and found Carolyn asleep. I touched her and then wedged into my side of the bed before falling asleep. The next morning was a Friday. We were both up yet walked gingerly around each other as if on tiptoe.

After getting ready for school, Carolyn said, "Bye, see you later."

I replied, "Yes, have a good day. When you get home, we need to talk."

She nodded.

That night, we talked for hours, zigzagging backward in time. We laughed about our mutual attraction during the summers when we were in high school. The dash I made from Houston Street to Cambridge and back, the return with Carolyn. I quickly named Edison, Rosie, and Lola as primary influences in my life. However briefly I knew them, they accepted me, took me in, loved Carolyn. Edison, in particular, urged us to get married without further ado.

He hoped for harmony, but Carolyn found his suggestion to be dissonant. She felt, early on, we were pushing too hard, too soon. I smiled and reminded her of Moab, and she softened for a moment. It was campy and we never left the motel, except for food. Carolyn, in the present, advocated spending more time together both as a couple and with others. As a duo, we never did break. Sometimes, we tipped over fairly steeply, but we ultimately held together.

Carolyn said we were like one of those old cars we had: fastened together with gum and rubber bands but somehow operational. This time I raised my eyebrows and mentioned that period, after Diana left, when Carolyn and I, by increments, moved further apart. We each found separate spots within our three-story house. Carolyn's profession focused on the nuances of personal relationship. Me? Even then, I could concentrate well only part of the time. The unspoken question was this: Would we uncouple?

We went away together to one of Carolyn's relative's unoccupied cottages on the Connecticut side of Long Island Sound. It was located in Waterford, where playwrights gather each summer to redo and fix scripts. We drove to the little house, which sat across the street from the water. It was midsummer, so we needn't worry about invading gusts of cold air. Warm and humid, the weather matched our moods. We made nothing but small talk as we drove from New Jersey to the Connecticut shore.

Then, torrents of feelings. I had disconnected. No, it was she who had become consumed with work. I had made excuses for leaving the house if not the bedroom. She had brought her work home. I was more interested in learning to play the piano than having a meal together. She liked her peers better than me.

We took a pause when it came to our children; each agreed that the other was a sensational parent. It was toward each other that Carolyn and I had become inert if not disregarding.

The few days by the sea drew us together. I recall walking separately and then Carolyn taking my hand. We returned to suburban New Jersey cautiously hopeful. She was ahead of me. I was considering the idea of seeing a therapist. But when I brought it up, I was surprised to learn that Carolyn felt we should first try working through things by ourselves. I imagined, given her intuitive sense, that she would welcome a third party.

The navigation was not always smooth: We spent months pushing and pulling, rediscovering, and then isolating again. Gradually, we began to look forward to a different chapter with each other. We were no longer irrefutably, mutually attracted twenty-two-year-olds, but we wanted to save our marriage.

"It's in the process, Harry," she said. "We will adapt."

Together

Already fatigued, Harry and Carolyn began the trek from Nevada to Utah. The enduring daylight enabled them to gaze at the topography and colors of the Southwest: the hues of browns and reds and a sky filled with deepening blue and then some scarlet as well. Out of the city, the rocks were jagged and resolute. Each cluster pronounced isolation. Harry and Carolyn were determined to drive straight through. It was too late to even consider stopping at a canyon.

They drove and drove, stopping only once at an all-night truck stop where they could get gas and use the restrooms before switching drivers and setting out once again. After six hours, they finally arrived on Main Street in Moab. A large, tall sign announcing Expedition Lodge beckoned. They had decided to spend just one night by themselves before meeting the daughters the next morning and then going to the house. It was well past midnight when Harry and Carolyn pulled in. The receptionist at the front desk, they later decided, was either on drugs or had slept all day in preparation for her shift. "What can I do for you?" she asked.

"We'd like a room for just tonight," said Carolyn.

"Sure," said the clerk. "Breakfast between 6 and 8:30. The fitness room opens at 8:00 and the pool an hour later. Coffee always and morning muffins out in the lobby. Treats in the afternoon. Okay?"

"Yeah, that's great," said Harry. "Thank you."

They grabbed their suitcases from the car, found the first-floor room, and fiddled with the key card until it let them in. Carolyn thought of trying to undress but then joined Harry by removing her shoes and jeans before diving under the covers.

Younger Generation

Marissa thought it best that just she and Diana, not the boyfriends for now, meet up with their parents. She couldn't decide whether an activity, like an easy walk, was a good idea or a bad one. She chose a pond she knew that was nearby. It had some benches and a small beach area. If anyone wanted to wade in, that was an option.

Remembering her parents' preferences for coffee, Marissa stopped in town, bought four iced coffees, wedged them into a tray, and then went to get Diana. Everyone wanted the family reunion to succeed, but it had been half a dozen years. Success was not a sure thing.

Marissa, driving, said to Diana, "Being an hour away from them the past few years, I gradually found out more about them. Mom told me it was hard after you left. Well, first I left and then you did. They didn't do too well."

"What do you mean?" Diana asked. "Did someone have an affair?"

"I don't know. It's not like they sat with me to explain it all. I'm not sure they're finished trying to get to this new normal stage."

"Is it possible," asked Diana, "that they wanted to get together to actually talk about everything? I mean, with their daughters?"

"I suppose. You want my take? It's like they were stuck in the past. It's not erasing the past but kind of making puzzle pieces of their lives fit now. I better watch where I'm going," said Marissa, "or I'll drive right past the place."

"They've known each other since high school. That's pretty close to fifty years. I am nowhere near understanding who I was then. And no steady boyfriend to even consider."

"And, as you probably noticed in high school, I was mostly trying to brush away guys who were after me for one thing," said the older sister. "Hey, we're close. When do you think they'll get here?"

"They just got in last night. It might take a few more minutes," said Diana. "I'm just glad LG isn't here. He's a handful."

"We, the two of us, Diana, should spend some time together after this. There's a lot to discuss, isn't there?" Marissa said and edged into a parking space.

"I had to leave," said Diana as a snappy-looking white car pulled up beside them.

"Hey," said Harry, bumping his head as he opened the driver-side door. "We have mini-SUVs back home; I'm not used to a low roof." He spread his arms, and Diana ran into them. At the same moment, Marissa greeted her mother with a careful yet caring hug.

"My first baby," said Carolyn.

"Mom, where's the music coming from?" Diana asked.

"Oh, man. I was in such a hurry to get out, I forgot to turn off the car," said Harry. "I brought a few CDs for the trip from Vegas to here. It's from *17 Tracks*, an obscure Springsteen album. This is 'Janey Don't You Lose Heart.'"

"I guess that's one thing we have in common. You passed on the Bruce gene," Marissa said as Diana danced to the tune. Carolyn, laughing, joined her and mouthed the words.

"Your father has forgotten that song came out in the mid-1980s. It was originally a track from *Glory Days*. Girls, always pay attention to detail," said Carolyn. "You two know that I used to sing, sometimes even with Dad, right? It started during a summer and blossomed during the short time in the East Village. We did get to a few places for open mic."

"Mom, what's going on?" Marissa asked.

"We don't really know why we're all here," added Diana. "You said it was time for the family to get together."

"Neither of you was ever very good at small talk," said Harry. "It's the same for me and your mom. So I guess we ought to get right to it."

"You're not splitting up, are you?" Marissa asked.

"No," said her mother, "but the story of how we've come back together might be helpful at some point."

"What is it then?" Diana asked. "You both look good, more like people in your mid-fifties than early sixties."

"I don't have early onset Alzheimer's," said Harry. "But something's not right, and they haven't figured out what it is. My memory just isn't what it used to be. Maybe I can just pin this on the time I fell on the tennis court and smacked my head."

"When was that?" Marissa asked.

"Maybe six months ago," said Carolyn. "He's been checked, and doctors are not clear on what's going on. I think unless they can tack it up on a bulletin board as a known condition, well, you get a fudge job. I mean, without a specific reason, people come up with cloudy responses. I know—we are pros at this in counseling. I have read that a major shock to the head, to the brain—as in a concussion—can lead to memory loss. After a traumatic accident, sometimes a person cannot even recall what happened."

"Not so in my case," said Harry. "Unbelievably, I tripped myself. I hate to admit it, control freak that I am, but that is indeed what happened."

"We're trying to deal with the situation, and we wanted to talk in person. This place is special for us," said Carolyn.

"One memory I won't give up," said Harry.

"So you were never a druggie, Dad?" said Marissa.

"After you left for college, Issa, he would have, like, a glass of wine two or three times a week," Diana said. ".At the club, though, that was different."

"I crashed on the tennis court," Harry said. "Ever since, well, I've had issues."

"It gets more complex because there isn't a lot of consistency," said Carolyn. "Sometimes, he's perfectly fine for a while. Then he'll forget more than the usual. It's okay for people our age to go to the store and totally blank on a few things. It's not okay if you can't remember, from before breakfast till way later, that you were supposed to go food shopping. It's happened. Then, he will be fine and you wouldn't know anything's up. In fact, we keep hoping that this could go away or slow to a crawl. He's fine on specifics from the distant past, actually more accurate on details involving you two than I am. As you can imagine, living in metro New York, we've been to some of the best people already. They say it's not dementia, which I guess is a silver lining."

Harry stood straighter. "Look, I'm me. Something's wrong inside of me, but I feel fine. Look at me. We planned this trip because it seemed a good time just to get together, not because of what your mother just said."

"Dad," said Diana, "I'm sure you remember that time when I was about fourteen and I wouldn't speak to Marissa."

"You could cut the tension between you like a scalding serrated blade running through butter. Yes."

"Good one, Har," said Carolyn.

"Obviously, we calmed down," said Diana.

"But we became closer the farther away we were from each other," said Marissa.

"I guess I pushed it to an extreme by moving across the country," said Diana.

"Obviously, we've been seeing Marissa every so often. An hour away isn't so far," said Carolyn.

"Sometimes," Harry added.

"I would come home every so often for a meal or even a good rest," said Marissa. "Listen, this is probably as good a time as any for me to say that I knew something was wrong."

"What? You never said a word to me, Issa," said Diana.

"At first, it was just a feeling I had," Marissa answered. "All of us know they were never the kind of people who are all over each other. The embarrassment for the two of us would have been . . ."

". . . impossible to deal with," said Diana.

"Still, it just seemed they were sometimes moving in opposite directions," Marissa said.

"We always loved each other," said Carolyn.

"When you're married forever, there are mountains and valleys," said Harry. "And if you're each following a different trail through the woods, something can go wrong."

"In our case, empty nest was edging toward broken nest," Carolyn said. "Now this."

"As you used to say to both of us, Mom, you're circling around. Do you need something?" Marissa asked.

"If I get worse, she—no, we—will need somebody," said Harry. "Not now, but maybe eventually the playing field will tilt and Mom could face carrying more than her fair share."

Diana said, "I'm the one who lives out here, but, honestly, I'm not attached to a job. I know the town, so I get work. I do have LG, but some space might be just what that relationship needs. I don't want to get into any more than that here. Want to go for a walk? As long as we're talking about trails, I know a lovely one around the other side of the pond. It doesn't have a name, but I've gone hiking on it before. It gives me time to tap into the introvert part of me," she continued. "Sometimes, I like to be by myself just to muse and wonder and consider. This place encourages all that."

Everyone followed Diana, but no one said a word until Harry piped up. "Always good to explore a new place," he said. "I've never been here, and neither has your mother. It is beautiful, and it isn't crowded." Then he added, "At least, I don't remember coming here." No one responded, and Harry chuckled. "That's me trying for some gallows humor," he said.

Carolyn tried to smile; no one else laughed.

Diana kept up a good pace with Marissa closely behind or, when the path permitted, beside her little sister.

"Wait," said Marissa, holding onto Diana's wrist and turning around to their parents, who were several yards behind.

"Look, that's sweet," she said when she saw that Harry and Carolyn were holding hands. "Since when do you do that?" she asked.

"Since after the diagnosis," said Carolyn, "about six months back."

"December 1, about a week after Thanksgiving. I have no trouble recalling events and exact dates," Harry said.

"Dad, the next part is kind of steep. Do you think you can do it?" Diana asked.

"That's just it. Physically, aside from a few sore joints, I am mensch-plus," he said. "I don't really understand why something is kaflooey up here, but I'm the poster child of my age group for many gymnastic-style activities."

"Sorry, dear," said Carolyn, "but one has nothing to do with the other. Well, being fit is always helpful, but beyond that . . . Incidentally, the doctors asked your father if he would participate in a new trial. The hospital is in the city, so it's local."

"Starting when?" Diana asked.

"A couple of weeks from now," answered Harry. "It begins with hypnosis, and I agreed."

For the next few days, six of them spent time together, with Grant and LG joining them on occasion. They walked, talked, and ate at a variety of restaurants. For the most part, Harry's medical predicament became a taboo topic. Harry and Carolyn, relieved that they'd flown out to share the news in person, continued, then backed off.

Marissa and Diana did address it the day after the pond hike. Marissa and Grant were staying in the spare bedroom where Diana lived. LG had his own apartment but spent some overnights with Diana at the parents' place. The average temperature for mid-June was in the low eighties, and, on this day, that was the case. The sisters chose the Moab Diner.

As they pulled up, Marissa said, "Good and familiar. Maybe the one we used to go to back home was more upscale with the fancy seats and all, but you can't really take the diner out of diner. Know what I mean?"

"I really didn't want to go to a bistro," said Diana.

Marissa, imitating Harry, said, "Eggs look and taste like eggs, no matter what."

Diana, laughing, said, "It's sort of true, but around here it's almost like the seasoning is different than it is back home."

"I know," said Marissa, "New York tastes different than Moab. So, what do you think? Where do we go from here?" she asked as they seated themselves in a corner booth.

"It's time for me to head east," said Diana.

Part IV

Chapter 8

New Jersey

July 2011

DIANA WAS SURPRISED TO find that she was happy to be back in northern New Jersey. She recalled her glory days as a teenage runner and tennis player. The high school, reputed to be academically superior, was fine rather than exceptional. Everyone was rich, or that's the way it seemed to her. Her best experiences were the times she spent outside running or playing. Now, she found more parks, bike paths, and walking and running trails than she remembered.

As a kid, she also liked books and art. The Barnes & Noble proved a tonic for her in that she could read as well as grab pastries and coffee if she so chose. There was nothing like that in Moab these days. And River Hill Art Park: sculpture, visual artistry, ceramics, glass blowing, and much more. Besides, she remembered nighttime jazz and some Shakespeare productions taking place there as well. Back when she was in high school, Marissa would bring her to music and plays. Now, Diana, feeling ready, took the initiative.

Obviously, this was not foreign turf for Marissa, who lived in Brooklyn but would hang out, from time to time, at her childhood home. The town was too fancy for her, and she wondered if it was also too upscale for her parents, who weren't very ostentatious. Yet these tiny bedroom villages were alluring in that they were safe and offered some culture. Besides, it only took an hour or so to get into the city. No wonder people were flocking here and to surrounding communities.

As both the big sister and the oldest child, Marissa felt a responsibility to and for everyone else in the family. Hearing of her dad's medical situation worried and even frightened her. She dreaded a firm prognosis. What if this disease turned out to be gradually debilitating? Where would that leave her mother? If it took years, could they all deal with bearing witness to her mother's slow decline? She doubted so.

Diana was staying at the house. Marissa still lived in her small apartment in Cobble Hill, Brooklyn, but she started spending long and longer weekends in New Jersey. She missed Grant, off designing a set, but spoke with him often. She knew he would come to visit and that might happen soon. Diana was ambivalent about LG. He seemed to be changing for the better, but, out there by himself, he could just revert and slide backwards.

The sisters, together, talked strategy about an illness no one had been able to fully identify yet, let alone understand. They also worried about their mother. Marissa was close by, close enough, when

her parents navigated through this anxiety ridden episode. Carolyn told her elder daughter just
enough. Harry tended to call on "his baby," the
younger daughter, Diana, should he need a listener.

While others spoke of summer heat, Diana felt
thankful for cooler nights in comparison to the
Southwest. She had grown accustomed to dry
heat, but sleeping in Moab without air conditioning always presented a challenge. Here, thirty miles from the city, she could open the two
windows in her childhood bedroom, turn on the
fan, and drift off.

Labor Day Weekend—Two Months Later

Everyone agreed that a family gathering for
the holiday, with Harry in charge as he always
had been, was in order. After all, it had been a
tradition forever, having evolved from being just
their insular unit to including friends and loved
ones, not to mention some wonderful music. This
time, though, it would be a family of four.

Marissa made the trip to spend the long weekend in the suburbs, which enabled the sisters
to revisit the past during late-night talks. After
drinking some wine with their parents, who finally went upstairs, the young women looked at one
another and started to laugh.

"I'm amazed they finally gave it up," Marissa
said when she was certain Harry and Carolyn
were out of earshot.

Diana added, "They're how old and he has something that's serious and, basically, they might have more stamina than we do, Issa."

"How can Dad be so strong and yet have whatever this thing is inside his head somewhere?"

"Issa, I'm afraid that someone's going to stick him or mess with his brain or something," said Diana.

"I heard them discussing Chinese medicine, which might involve ginkgo. They said something about Danshen root, which I've never heard of," Marissa said.

"In my mind, I was afraid they would go to something way more harmful like electroshock. I base this on nothing other than that I'm fearing the worst." Diana paused. "I've done acupuncture. How about you?"

"Yes, performing sometimes beats my body, and I tried it to calm my whole physical system and nerves, too."

"And mine worked," said Diana, "way back with high-level road racing, which trashes your joints. I found someone good when I was in high school. For all I know, she's still in this town."

"You know how Dad was working for a long time in a jazz club? He really loved both the music and how cozy the place was. It typically doesn't bring in incredible top artists, but every so often a good one gets booked. One time, they brought in Kenny Barron to play piano. I did not know the name, but Dad called me to say he thought Barron lived in Brooklyn. I still don't know if that's true, but I did find out he's taught at Julliard and Rutgers."

Diana's mind wandered, and she wondered whether she'd missed out on more than she imagined by moving a few thousand miles away. This place, on a certain level, suited her. Marissa knew their parents better. She, still the little sister, was a lengthy plane ride away, while Marissa was just an hour away.

"What does all of this have to do with Dad's illness or the future?" Diana asked.

"It's the six-degrees thing," said Marissa. "Barron often played and recorded with Stan Getz and, in fact, did that right before Getz died of cancer. When Barron came to the club, according to Dad, he talked about Getz doing Eastern medicine, like herbs and leaves, and for a while stopping the disease. The connection here is maybe the ginkgo and Dad possibly understanding that Getz was okay for a period but then dreadfully not."

"I get it," said Diana. "I want them to talk to me, even more often, about it. It's possibly transforming all of their lives and each of them is reading, researching."

Marissa said, "That's probably good. I think they might actually be searching rather than researching. To change the subject totally, want to go for a walk around the block?"

"Sure," said Diana. "What time is it—10:00, 10:30? Think anyone's still up in bedroom-community America?"

It was chilly enough, on an early September night, to need sweatshirts, and these they found in an old toy chest that had never been moved, let alone touched, since they had left home. It was mahogany and wedged into a corner of Diana's childhood room. It opened with a creak, and they found similar cardigans from their teenage days.

"Our favorite colors," said Marissa. "You were always blue, and I couldn't be like you so for me it was forest green."

"Nothing like the Southwest reds and browns I'm used to," said Diana. "The landscape is softer here, but I'm not sure which I like better."

Residents turned out lights as the sisters walked past houses. It was as if eleven at night was a cutoff. The homes, themselves, were not uniform. They were large, and many were old. All of the neighbors, however, seemed to agree that it was time to call it a day.

Diana said, "The stars, though, jump out at you in Moab. Here, they're settled back, even passive."

Marissa threaded her arm through her sister's and suddenly asked, "Have you heard them talking about MS?"

"Not exactly, no. But I know that Dad's been doing some meditating and deep breathing. They exercise together sometimes, and that never used to be true. They even do yoga."

"Wow," said Marissa. "All to hold Dad's brain right here in the present."

"If they start that thing with lists as reminders," said Diana, "I'm going to think of Alzheimer's and freak out."

"Dad does not seem to be funny, fuzzy, or vague. This weekend, for instance, he has it all together. This is an old-style Dad party; that's how it seemed at dinner tonight," said Marissa. "Hey, look, it's Croydon's house, and it hasn't changed much since we were little."

In a nifty neighborhood, one home stood apart since it was unkept, uncared-for. Many shingles were loose, and the exterior was never finished. Mrs. Croydon, when they came for trick-or-treat, would always say, "Paint and wood, no good," which made everyone laugh. She was thin-lipped, and her neck veins popped when she spoke. Her goal, thought the sisters, was to terrorize children or maybe she was pretending. Now they came face-to-face with the haunted house and its owner. Surprisingly, the outside light was on and the interior, too, was illuminated by lamps.

Diana asked, "What, exactly, caused us to be terrified of her when we were kids?"

"We decided she was like a scarecrow. She was all bones and scrawny, remember?"

"Did we just make stuff up about her in our heads? We thought she was ninety years old back in the day. Obviously, we were totally off," said Diana.

"It's possible that she's just more interesting than everyone else around here, like Mom and Dad's friends," said Marissa. "I bet if we looked inside, we could almost feel energy in there."

"Let's just go around the block, okay?" was Diana's response. They resumed walking, along with their previous conversation about Harry. "Sooner or later," Diana said, "we have to stop circling around Dad's situation."

"Yes. The two of us have to quit dancing around the two of them. Sure, they're our parents, but we're adults," said Marissa.

❧ ❧

Upstairs, Harry and Carolyn had come upon a trove of photos from that formative summer of 1970. At the time, Harry thought he might become a journalist and that it would be wise to be able to take some pictures. Now they held sweet memories of Edison, Rosie, and Lola; the brief time in Cambridge; the return to Houston Street, this time with Carolyn; and, finally, Moab.

Back then, Harry carried his camera wherever he went. Whatever afflicted him did not disturb these sharp visual memories. There were two photos of them together. One was in front of the Utes Motel, where he had asked the friendly clerk to snap a shot of them. The justice of the peace, too, was kind enough to take a picture of them just after the short wedding ceremony. There it was: resplendent, even on faded glossy paper, forever.

As was their relationship, which traversed that period when each went semi-solo. Neither had abandoned the other, but rather each had created a separate sphere in which to exist. The Waterford weekend had brought them back together.

Carolyn's Segue: She

Harry, the journalist, and she, the guidance counselor, began to make parallel lists: Alzheimer's, MS, Parkinson's, Lewy disease. Perhaps the sum total of any of those parts meant some form of dementia.

Harry was terrified yet accepting. He had survived through his early sixties, loved his wife and daughters, cobbled together various careers. In all, he was one fortunate soul. Carolyn, on the other hand, was terrified and unaccepting. She had never been one to give in, always claimed her will would take her through, and now she demanded that Harry's quality of life continue. She would figure this out and carry them forward.

In the meantime, she intended to delay, if not forgo entirely, using tricks designed to jar Harry's memory. She was determined not to resort to notes and cards and stickers to remind Harry who he was and where he lived. She wasn't about to mount photographs of Marissa, Diana, and herself on the walls just in case Harry became confused. He was nothing like that—at least, not yet.

But deep inside, she wondered if she could survive, whether she had the fortitude to cope or if she would collapse. She dreaded a mentally diminished Harry, someone she did not know. For all of her service work, she could not imagine the level of care Harry's predicament might require. She was aware that she would never be prepared for that.

Monday Party

Harry knew he could manage this, and he desperately wanted to show his daughters and, most of all, Carolyn that he was still himself. Atmosphere was everything. They had bought the house because it included two back lots. They had invested in landscaping early, then learned to do it themselves. This was a project he and Carolyn initiated, maintained, enjoyed together. Harry wasn't much for indoor cards or games, but he loved turning the dirt over in his hands and Carolyn preached communion with nature as the ultimate therapy. Horticulture was a mutually engaging joy. So what if he couldn't recall the name of each plant? He could still tell an oak from a maple tree.

Setting up the canopy in early afternoon, Harry brought his two-CD Gershwin Platinum Collection to accompany him as he hung crepe paper streamers from the tent's midpoint to the ground in a neatly symmetrical pattern. He would show them. He reveled in listening to Judy Garland sing "But Not for Me" soon after the first disc began. He had defended Garland forever, claiming that she was a victim of her talent, her openness, and the unrealistic expectations that followed after "Over the Rainbow" came out. Harry sang along as Carolyn, smiling, watched from the expansive kitchen sliding doors that led outside. He then turned off the player.

He'd grown up listening to his father's Glenn Miller and Duke Ellington LPs, and as he grappled with a potentially clouded future, Harry turned to the music. Many times, he had admonished his thirteen-year-old self for giving up on alto sax. Maybe it wasn't cool to be in a jazz band, but he loved that teacher and the way he cajoled them to practice. Harry could not believe he had traded that potential for a first baseman's glove and, eventually, a spot on the ninth-grade baseball team.

Fortunately, working at the club in Montclair had given him a chance to hear great saxophonists like Coleman Hawkins, Lester Young, Ben Webster, and John Coltrane since the place had a stash of old LPs and a high functioning turntable. His personal favorite was Stan Getz. Now, he placed a disc of Getz touring somewhere in Europe in the CD player and pressed play. Harry wondered how, given his recent issues, he could recall these details with perfect ease. This was, according to Kenny Barron, the piano player, the last Getz concert. At the time, Stan had cancer, had tried treatments, and was going for a new, experimental one. Harry remembered reading all about this in liner notes. Then Harry stopped for a minute, frozen in place. When he snapped to, he wondered just where was that the aluminum spatula he used for the grill?

Harry collected caps that sported the names of beaches, some of which he and Carolyn had visited. The one he was wearing said Miami and had a single palm tree beside the name. They had gone there, as a family, and even the girls had tolerated it. They were old enough that he and Carolyn felt comfortable letting them go off by themselves for evening ocean walks. The situation was ideal.

This was an Indian summer day, which suited him: He always craved heat. He had the usual burgers and chicken, but, by now, he was the only one who looked forward to meat for dinner. Carolyn acquiesced, Marissa would rather not, and Diana didn't eat much of anything. He had plenty of salads, too, both veggie and fruit. That would complement the traditional barbecue.

Have-it-together Harry. That was him. Even when feeling discombobulated, he was able to feign composure. He would show them by organizing a themed event. Thus, the hat. The warm and muggy weather was nothing if not beach-like. Hence, Harry had his cache of Beach Boys CDs ready for later. He had the one called *The Beach Boys Today!* It included one of his favorites, "Help Me Rhonda," which he and Carolyn used to sing together all the time. If he could still remember the lyrics and sing, he must be fine.

The music was set, but he needed utensils and platters. Harry was determined not to ask where he could find these things, yet he was temporarily stumped. He wandered up the deck stairs, spread open the sliding glass doors, and found a smiling Carolyn awaiting him.

"I was watching you completely in your element, dear. Your preparation for these events, all these years, is almost equally delectable when compared to the actual festivity," she said as she pushed Harry's cap higher onto his head. She took his face in both of her hands and kissed him.

He hugged her and said, "It's like I'm demonstrating to myself I can still do this." He refrained from saying more. "I would be hearing something if the girls were here. Where'd they go?"

"They said they were going to the mall to get special treasures for tonight, but I'm not sure I believe them," said Carolyn. "They were both wearing shoes that suggested otherwise—like, trekking sneakers or something. Listen, I was thinking maybe we could sing something, like we used to way back when, to impress the kids."

"You mean James Taylor or Carole King or Simon & Garfunkel? Sure."

"I was thinking along those lines at first, but then I stumbled over 'As Tears Go By' and I managed to play it on the piano while singing along. Here." Carolyn handed Harry the sheet music.

He laughed as he examined the cover. "Seventy-five cents to buy this in the mid-60s. I always thought Mick Jagger had written it, but now I see Keith Richards also gets some credit. Who is this third guy, Andrew Loog Oldham?"

"I had the same question, so I looked it up and discovered he was manager of The Stones for four years. Somehow, he has a credit on this song. Come on, let's try it. Just think of Edison and we'll be good."

"Oh yeah, that's someone I never forget," said Harry.

Carolyn began singing with compassion and drama.

"Appropriate choice, C. Let me try the harmony with you on just that," said Harry. But they didn't stop after they finished that part. As he held the music in front of them, they continued through the entire song.

"The only thing is this, Carolyn: Why choose one that ends with a person seated to watch tears?" Harry asked.

"I know," she said. "I wasn't looking for it, just pulled it out where it was stuck between books of music. It is sad but pretty, no?"

"Yes, although I prefer The Beach Boys, which is what will be on for tonight," he answered.

⁂

Marissa and Diana found their way to Eagle Rock Reservation in West Orange, which the family had visited a few times years ago. It wasn't all that far from the house, and Diana recalled that the views were amazing.

"I want to see the city where you live, Issa, from twenty miles away," Diana said as they pulled into a parking area. "Maybe you can spot your part of Brooklyn."

"Doubtful," Marissa said, "but let's walk along this part. All I know is that it's called Lenape."

Off they went before stopping, soon enough, to catch views of New York. Walking slowly, they saw the skyline, various bridges, and, on the other side, views of New Jersey communities.

"It's not the Southwest, but, in a way, it's much cozier," said Diana.

"There's some green," added Marissa. "You know, it's different to spend time just with you. The couple thing with LG and Grant, that was good to do in Moab, but I'm not sure I'd want to do it here."

"And who knows if there will be an LG in my life much longer?" said Diana. Her mind was divided: He was making an attempt; on the other hand, who was she to set up requirements? Maybe he just preferred to drink and laze around. She'd already expended so much energy toward trying to reform him.

"I miss Grant, sure, but he is not going away," said Marissa. "I try to picture him twenty or thirty years from now, and that's promising. I never picture anything more than the two of us, though."

"Like, no kids?" said Diana.

"Exactly. He is a soul mate, but I've not even imagined Grant as a dad."

"We'll have to continue this conversation later. Right now, we need to get back. Mom might still think we're at Short Hills Mall."

Extricating themselves from Eagle Rock was easy since all paths led back to the visitors' area.

As soon as Diana began driving, Marissa said, very directly, "Could you stay around here for a while, Diana?"

"Every time that enters my mind, I push it to the back," she said, "not because it's a bad idea but because my life is in Moab. Correction: It's *been* in Moab. To answer your question, I've been thinking about that, too. I would definitely need to have work. I don't know about staying in the house with Mom and Dad. It's fine for now, but that would be a lot in the long term. It's possible, though, that it makes sense for me to be around here."

Marissa said, "I'm an hour away, and my plan is to come here more often. What are we going to do if this turns out to be early Alzheimer's or something like that?" When Diana did not reply, Marissa continued, "I think we both know that we have to take care of them just like they always did with us."

"Always is right. We were their first priority," said Diana.

Soon enough, they were back at the house. They expected to find their father outside setting up for dinner. Instead, they heard voices combining on harmony inside the house as they came to the wraparound front porch.

"Like the old days," Marissa said. "James Taylor and Carole King singing 'You've Got a Friend.'"

"The perfect choice," said Diana. "Is there any chance all of this could bring them closer?"

Marissa shrugged her shoulders. She called out, "We're back! And before you ask, no, we did not go to the mall."

Harry and Carolyn, hand in hand, greeted their daughters.

Harry spoke first.

"Not that it's on anybody's mind," he said, "but still no word on what I officially have. To prove I was still sane, I dug out an old beach hat. Remember when we did winter vacation in Miami?"

"I actually found something through my research," said Carolyn.

"Both of us always watched in awe as you delved into whatever it was that interested you—recipes, natural cures for scrapes, meditation," said Marissa, joining hands with Diana.

Carolyn could not fully read whether the comment was meant to be gently sarcastic or sincere. She went on: "What I found is that a part of the brain gets stimulated by music. I think it brings back emotions and may help to provide an association with an occasion or time in life."

"While I have all or most of my marbles," Harry said, "let me add this part: It's what Carolyn and I shared, in different ways, since we came together. I hate to admit this, but if Mom has to deal with me a bit, music could make that smoother."

"Yeah, but you are completely yourself now, Dad. You don't really need to list music you love to create associations with people because . . ."

Marissa picked up the thought. ". . . you're just not there yet. From what you've told us, you guys used to sing in small clubs in the Village when you were younger than we are now. Naturally, it's pretty great to hear you do this, but it hasn't been proven that Dad's sick, Mom."

"Not in the scheme, no," said Harry. "The immediate plan is to have the very best Labor Day party in the history of this family."

And so it became, this time around, a Motown extravaganza: dancing to The Supremes, The Temptations, Smokey Robinson, Marvin Gaye, Mary

Wells, Stevie Wonder, and more. Finally, to cap it all off: James Brown. Everyone danced to the music and danced around Harry's predicament.

Diana asked, "Wasn't this the best Labor Day ever? Dad's outdone himself and, honestly, everyone else who lives in this town," she declared.

No one argued; everyone hugged and raised a final glass of sangria as Carolyn said, "It's the best of times."

Harry Reflects: 2

I first made a journal entry forty-one years ago around Labor Day, when I couldn't figure out my life. Then two more within days. Here I am again, writing down my thoughts. I made a choice long ago, and it worked out. Marriage is forever. I might not have all my faculties as I contemplate another decision: Do I want to stick around as the gears in my brain entangle and ultimately crash?

Or should I say crunch—is that more vivid and sensory? Perhaps the various tentacles snap, crackle, and pop just like the cereal. No one seems to know or wants to say or comes clean with an honest assessment. Best case is this: The degeneration might be slow, which would enable me, potentially, to live a longer and fuller life.

I can compromise if the huge part of me is, well, still Harry, idiosyncrasies and all. We all know I haven't had a major career fulfillment, but I did manage to cobble together interests if not passions: music and journalism. Yes, I've been able to balance writing and listening. Taken together, it's been sustaining. So, I thought, I'm going to document this journey through my iPhone. I figure this will help me and maybe many others, too. I'm far from tech-savvy, but I know enough to be able to combine my voice with music through recordings.

I can make this a game: Carolyn and the girls get clues and guess what music I'm thinking about. And then I'll sing it. I've always been best in the family at remembering lyrics. We'll see if this changes if whatever condition I have is harmful. Before, we were singing "As Tears Go By," which is easy for me to remember. I will quiz myself in a while, which could reveal quite a lot.

What if I can't put on my socks? What if I confuse socks with shoes? What if I cannot drive? Having to be fully dependent on Carolyn is unacceptable. At least I am currently able to process this.

It is the dream, the visual which recurs, that disturbs me: My brain is engulfed within a network of overlapping spiderwebs. Really. I climb up and in to destroy them or clear the space, and I fail. When the lighting shifts from a medium gray toward black, I wake myself up. Scary.

Ultimately, it is the unknown that shakes me. I've always been a control freak, but people often do not notice behind the veneer of Mr. Mellow. Co-workers always talk about how unfazed I am, but it's really a defense mechanism. I don't want people to realize how I really feel when I'm frightened. I've been told to ease up on, if not give up, the facade. Maybe this is the time to push harder for that.

Would it be worse to not be able to find a lawn-mower or use one? Let's say I have some kind of mind deficiency. I still have fine motor skills, but I cannot use them. With the other kind of thing, like Parkinson's, I can tell where everything is, but, for example, at a certain point I cannot balance myself on a bicycle.

I probably need to spend some time with a person I trust whose name is not Carolyn. Who would that be? I wonder if Edison is still in the city. I remember him in great visual detail, his apartment on Houston, all of it. Yes, we did keep up for a while. After moving out here, we wrote and called and went into the city every so often. He would have Rosie and Lola over, and it was the same as it was back in 1970: food, drink, fun, some music. But eventually, that went away, slowly ebbed, till it was no more. Anyway, maybe crazy, eccentric Edison has more advice for me. He kicked me in the ass the first time. At the very least, I should try to find him.

The real question is how. I don't have a cell number for him. We do have his old home phone number in the address binder. Yeah, I can start with that if I can only remember where it is. And we never did know his last name, so I don't have to worry about remembering that. I only know him as Edison.

Perhaps it would be easier if Carolyn went with me. Not as chancy. No. I need to find him, see him, myself.

Calling Edison

Harry, a hoarder, kept the ancient address book at the bottom of an old carton labeled "H Findings" in the attic. He found Edison's phone number scribbled on the front cover. When he tried it, a familiar voice answered not with a hello but with a question: "For love or money?"

"Love. It's Harry, Edison. You know, from back in the day. I'd . . . Would it be possible for me to come see you?"

Edison knew who it was immediately. "What I always liked about you, young man, is that you race to the chase, never mind cut."

"I'm over sixty," said Harry, "so I'm not such a young man anymore."

"Back then, I must have been a dozen or fifteen years your senior. I suppose that's still true," said Edison.

Harry had never asked but figured Edison was in his mid-sixties back in 1970—which was nowhere near the truth.

"When will you be here? Still with gorgeous?" Edison asked.

"Tomorrow? The next day? And yes—even if I do not deserve her," Harry said.

"Come Wednesday for early dinner. I'll get Rosie to come. Lola lives in Connecticut now. Are you bringing your lovely bride or showing up solo?"

"Solo," Harry said. "Are you still at 24 East Houston?"

"Yes. It's condos now but mostly the same. I can tell you more once you get here," said Edison. "Are you bringing a guitar?" Before Harry could answer, Edison added, "I still have my menagerie of instruments and more. Music is the bridge from one era to the next, don't you agree?"

"I didn't know if I would find you, Edison," said Harry. "Man, you blow me away."

<hr>

Harry recalled a scruffy Edison who was perpetually on the verge of looking disheveled and unkempt. Now, that same man welcomed Harry into his living space with a handshake and then a close hug. Edison had grown his instrument collection since 1970, and it was organized according to type: woodwinds, strings, percussion, and a sleek-looking black electric piano.

"Look," said Edison, "I've made some changes, especially in the kitchen." Edison ushered Harry into that room, where the face of each cabinet showed a black-and-white photo of a musician. "Catch these," continued Edison. "I actually took those two. Jazz guys: McCoy Tyner and Lee Konitz. They play in clubs, and you can sometimes get close enough to shoot, even talk with, them. Taking these pictures, that's become another passion for me. I can see what they're trying to do, and I can spend hours here practicing."

"Hello, Edison," said Harry, and the older man smiled.

"Guess I was jumping ahead, which happens when you live by yourself. You have a visitor and just start spewing forth. Harry, you don't look the same," he said.

"I was a confused kid back then," said Harry.

"Perhaps so, but also wildly talented and bright." Edison paused. "No Rosie or Lola this time, but they're in for the next time—and there will be a next time. What brings you here after a hundred years of no see, no talk, no hear from?"

Harry, seeing that this man, now somewhere in his late seventies, bore great resemblance to his younger self, began to relax. "How are Rosie and Lola?" he asked, evading the question.

"Rosie and Richard bought Lola's apartment—I mean, condo—when she left. Sometimes, their kids live there; sometimes they rent it out. Lola got married, moved to Connecticut, then divorced. She is often the one back in her old place, but now as a visitor. And what about you? You have children who are older than you were when you first knocked on my door, don't you?"

"Yes. One lives in Brooklyn, the other in Moab out in Utah," said Harry. "Both have been here for the past few weeks. I guess you could say they're here for me."

"Come clean, Harry. What's going on?"

Harry walked from the living room to the kitchen and back. "I remember it looking sort of like this forty years ago, Edison. You've got some newer woodwinds and shinier horns and you've bought a few more things, but not many. They're artifacts. Like me. A period piece out of a specific era. I mean, you were here when the Beats were in the Village. I got to be a small part of that, thanks to you. You took Carolyn and me to the open mic nights, and artsy folks were always there sitting around, drinking, smoking, talking. You see, I have vivid and visual recall of that. I'm losing something, though. That's why it seems the right word for me is artifact—because I'm stuck in the past."

"You were such a quick study, Harry, and always eager for suggestions, even criticism. So level with me: You keep talking about memory, which means what?" Edison asked.

"I don't have an exact diagnosis. The easiest way to describe it, I guess, is to say that upon occasion, I simply cannot remember things. Nada. Other times, I have sharp recall. My parents' generation would write this off with 'go figure,' but I cannot. The situation drives me insane because, for the most part, I'm with the program."

"More music, Harry," said Edison. "Ancient poets and more recent ones, like Dylan, write lyrics that we then memorize. It even goes beyond that for me. There's been an assimilation: Music is a part of my being. I know that sounds almost fraudulently psychological, but it becomes part of my chemistry—a mixture of art and science, I say."

"Since we last saw each other . . . Check that. Since I lost my friendship with you, one of the things I've been doing is working in a jazz club: listening, talking into the night with musicians—just becoming a sponge that soaks it all in."

"You know, then, that the jazz greats often spent all day and all night just getting one chord sequence where they want it. Coltrane, Sonny Rollins . . . they're known for that. Part of that, for sure, is that they have a gift. But it's also mind work. Come here," said Edison, leading Harry to the electric piano. He then played and sang every word of Tom Paxton's "The Last Thing on My Mind."

"I remember it well, Edison. You took Carolyn and me to listen to Paxton at Gerde's Folk City."

"Music recall is the stimulus, and you know the beginning portion of the lyrics before the part I just did," said Edison. "It's my theory that music can be a preservative and possibly even encourage life. Of course, I cannot prove this scientifically. Tell me more about what's going on with you."

"To use a phrase that is a blast from the past, I think we're all freaking out: Carolyn, me, our daughters. We often try to pretend all is well. But what if I . . . what if my mind does just go away with no word of farewell?"

Edison did not answer directly. Instead, he picked up a guitar and launched into a folk song medley. He was a deft guitarist whose voice was more than adequate, less than stellar. He encouraged Harry to join him, and they harmonized (after Edison had finished with some Beatles) on Paxton's 'Ramblin' Boy.'"

"Next time, I will have Rosie here and I'll ask Lola if she can come, too. I would love to see Carolyn."

"Yes, you will," replied Harry. He and Edison hugged as Harry realized he'd made the right decision to visit this formative figure of a past life. Edison had his theories, and his strong belief in them was infectious. As Harry got into his car, he was thinking about music. He couldn't wait to see Carolyn and share what Edison had said.

Carolyn, sinking deep into the hammock and swinging gently over the front porch boards, eagerly awaited Harry's return. "Tell me he hasn't changed in forty years," she said when he reached the front steps.

"Essentially the same singular, unpredictable dude," said Harry. "He thinks music could save me, had me singing a few Tom Paxton songs with him."

"Hey, Harry, you think Edison wants to revisit our trio? I mean, Dylan's still singing."

"Dylan has lost a lot of his voice but none of his talent," Harry said. He paused a moment before continuing, "And, as far as I know, his memory is intact."

"I've been doing some research on the brain—not only yours Harry, but mine, too. I've found the usual: do crossword puzzles; don't isolate yourself; even play video games, if you can believe that. All of the data says being physical helps, too. Nothing especially new. Relevant to what Edison said, though, at the bottom of one list and further up another is music. It's said that songs can get you to recall what happened years back. They're calling this musical memory and . . ."

Harry interrupted. "I've read about this, too, and how it improves quality of life. They use it in nursing homes. By the way, I'm not going to one, Carolyn. If it ever looks like that's where we're headed, get me pills instead, please."

"I wasn't trying to depress both of us," she answered. "They're talking about releasing the past through music to get the brain activated. The difference now is that you just can't nail down some specifics from more recent days and weeks. It's not that you're out of it entirely."

"Carolyn, let me get this right. I love that you're being so, so aggressive with this. Edison thinks music will jolt me, my brain, forward. Like it's all been slightly too stagnant for too long. I go back and forth. Sometimes, I think maybe but other times, skittish."

"Okay, someone thinks that learning a new instrument can awaken whatever it is in our brains that is equivalent to—and this is my image—embers that are gradually darkening. Think about that, Harry," said Carolyn. "For me, I never had enough air to blow into any instrument. What if I tried oboe or even trumpet? That would be fun and, since I have no expectations, whatever happened would be a plus."

"That's you, dear. You're not the one who suddenly blanks when asked to name four best friends from college. Me? Sure, I've always wanted to be in percussion—the guy in the back with the drum set and the weird eyes darting all over."

"Let's go buy a drum set, Harry. I can see you with one of your hats or even new ones for this occasion. That would be perfect. You could dress the part."

"Yes! Also, Carolyn, I think what Edison is suggesting is parallel. You know how from day one, way back, he loved our voices? By the way, he has instruments all over his place and I bet some are the same and some new. I'm going to speak for him, but I think he sees the human voice as, well, one of the greatest of all instruments. Imagine this: We see him and begin working on some tunes, just like we did back in 1970. We prepare for a gig, even if it's just singing at his place. Rosie and Lola could come—I'll give you what I know of them in a minute. Maybe Marissa and Diana could come, too. If it goes well, we do more. Doesn't that sound fun?"

"There's this little light, which I both know and treasure, in your eyes, Harry. Why not? Yes, to both: the drums and Edison," she said.

❧❧❧❧❧ ❧❧❧❧❧

"Sure, you're older but hardly different. Gray suits you," said Carolyn to Edison. She refrained from commenting on the women. If Rosie's features had softened, the opposite was true of Lola's. But both women sounded decades younger than their years as if in defiance of time spent on earth. When Carolyn thought of the old days, she recalled food, drink, and warmth; not much had changed there.

"I brought some goodies," Rosie said. "I hope you don't mind—chocolate cookies with the deep, rich bittersweet chips."

"I knew she would do something like that," Edison said. "Her pastries are perfecto with milk or seltzer. Can you imagine how happy old-world Jews trudging across Eastern Europe would have been if only they could have shared a hit? You can see my ladies do not age," he continued, bowing toward Lola and Rosie. "Rosie stayed the course with me here on Houston, but Lola went Gold Coast on me with her house in Connecticut."

"Ha!" said Lola. "A hut in Stamford is hardly the Taj Mahal, Ed. No, I got sucked in by a man who wanted someone to take care of him—the whole deal: cook, clean, sleep with. And the rewards were few: out to dinner once or twice a week, none of the trips or art events he so sincerely promised. Maybe I was just desperately searching and ended up being his attendant. I'm still wondering how I could be so gullible. Maybe I should move back to the building instead of living in plastic land."

"Without you, Lo, we're missing a vital third of the composite," said Edison.

"I guess I always think of all of you being on this same floor," Lola added. She gestured to Harry and Carolyn. "Even if you two were up above us. No matter. Edison said we needed to be here. Why?"

"I can't remember why," Harry replied, "is the issue, the problem, the nugget I cannot crack."

"He thought connecting with Edison could help, even though we don't have a diagnosis," said Carolyn. "I will say that after Harry visited Edison, he came back seeming more like the old Harry than a frightened, fretful man."

"Richard has dementia," said Rosie, silencing the room.

Harry spoke first. "I'm so sorry, Rosie," he said. "May I ask what that means?"

"He still knows me and the children, so far," she answered.

"He was always a bit of a mystery to me during that brief time I was on the scene, Rosie," said Carolyn. "Are you able to talk about it, or is it wrong for me to ask?"

"Maybe sharing the details will help you—both of you," said Rosie. "It seemed he lost it in a flash, but, looking back on the past two years, it happened more slowly than that. It was so minor in the beginning that we joked about it. He referred to his brother as whatchamacallit or said the underground when he meant the subway. That was funny, and we thought nothing of it. I think the first serious inkling that Richard was in trouble came when I sent him to the store and he was confused in the aisles. He called me on his flip phone and was befuddled." Rosie shook her head and stopped as Lola put her arm around Rosie's shoulders and then massaged her friend's neck.

Harry didn't hesitate. "What's the diagnosis, Rosie?"

"Not Alzheimer's, but it gets vague after that. I'm not sure they can give it an exact name, and, honestly, I don't care. He's slipping further away all the time, Harry. Are you okay?" Rosie asked.

Carolyn jumped in to answer. "Yes, he's still Harry," she said. "It's hard to determine whether this is a sixty-something-year-old with a senior moment coming on or a more serious condition. That said, we're both scared."

Edison tried to cut the tension. "Let's sing like we always did. Music therapy," he said. "How about some rounds of 'Swing Low, Sweet Chariot'? Remember when I had you two"—he nodded at Harry and Carolyn—"compose a love song with me? First, I sing, 'We are finally together and what do I see? Two swinging people so dear to me, comin' for to carry me home.'"

Then Harry jumped in with "I looked over Jordan and what did I see? Nurture and caring—a cocoon for me, comin' for to carry me home." Before anyone else lent lyrics, Harry took the floor: "Yes, I do feel scared but less so here. Thank heaven for that. Can I just say, before we sing some more, that I'm not certain if being here helps, but I do, as we all said in the old days, feel the love and it gives me hope. Not expectation but an optimism that this journey will not end with me submerged, no."

Carolyn picked up one of Edison's guitars and gently began to play the melody for "Swing Low" without singing a word. When she finished, she said, "Harry and I have always been such highly programmed people. We're not very spontaneous, which maybe kind of pushed our younger daughter, Diana, in that direction. Marissa, the older sister, is like us but also able to just get out of town if need be. I am not that good at dealing with the unknown, and neither is Harry."

Edison interrupted. "So, in other words, you want to corner and fix whatever ails Harry, and you cannot," he said.

"The doctors just do not say what it is," said Harry. "I could lead a relatively sane last quarter or third of my time on this planet, or I could end up institutionalized."

Suddenly from a perch on the wall, a cuckoo clock came to life with a series of calls. Rather than being synchronized, the noises were off beat. Harry and Carolyn looked at each other and laughed. They were joined by Lola and Rosie as Edison, always a puppet master, slyly grinned.

"It wasn't like that when I bought it," he said. "The bird, so to speak, came out at regular intervals and on the hour. It took me a long time to make it more imaginative."

"Eccentric, like you," said Harry. "Maybe I will be wacko like that. Or, since I am looking into reincarnation, maybe for my next gig I'll get to be a monkey. Except I'll sing instead of collecting coins—you know, I'll be the star and not the slave."

Rosie interrupted and said, "Harry, Richard started showing he was losing it years ago. We both denied it, but the kids, when he wasn't looking, told me he was going downhill. They did this because they were terrified. You are not that person. You're the same Harry. You have less hair and more lines on your face, but you're still sweet."

Motioning toward Edison, Lola said, "Let's eat and drink before this guy decides we ought to have a group sing at a local bookshop. He doesn't do open mic anymore, but before you know it, he'll have some ensemble soiree going."

She and Rosie went into the kitchen and brought out champagne and red wine, complemented by cheese and crackers. Rosie said, "I have a mean, unhealthy but delicious devil's-food cake at my place, which I will get for dessert."

As they sat down to eat, Edison said, "Four decades and you have these grown-up daughters. I'm glad I sent you off to Moab. Fill me in, what's happened?"

Harry and Carolyn provided a synopsis of life in a bedroom community just an hour away in northern New Jersey, the daughters who were dissimilar yet close, the recent trip back to Moab. They didn't expand on the time when their bond loosened but then returned with welcome warmth and understanding. All Carolyn said about that was, "We each drifted but, as you can see, stayed for the duration."

"Assuming I do not lose my mind, we carry on," said Harry. "Here we are. Carolyn's had a career counseling adolescents and teaching music, too—heroic work. I've cobbled together gigs at a local newspaper in the 'burbs with an evening job at a jazz club. A far cry from taking census as a sweating hippie in 1970 but also not exactly a prominent career path."

"Look at me," said Edison. "Itinerant music teacher, player of multiple instruments yet master of none, without enough shekels for retirement."

"Kindred brother," said Rosie.

"I still turn to you, which is probably why I'll leave Stamford for Houston Street as soon as I get myself together," added Lola. "During 1970, give or take, we thought this floor was communal and talked about gluing it together, if you know what I mean. That made Edison nervous, and he still has that. There is permanence in his life, but he sees himself as a vagabond."

"Gypsy sounds more romantic," said Edison. "I don't have kids and never see my family. I have home and you and these guys." He gestured around the living room toward all his instruments. "I've labeled each instrument just in case the Angel of Death comes in, having missed the mark on the front door telling her to skip us and move on. You know, like at Passover when the X on your apartment might save your life. Anybody for some Klezmer tunes?"

"Your mind is a hopping non sequitur, Edison," said Harry. "No problem for me to know this or to follow your dots and try to make them connect. I only wish I could be confident about my own memory carriers."

"You do not seem sick," said Rosie, going straight to it.

"He's not a total disaster but also not quite right," said Carolyn. "If only we could get it at least closer to quite right and forget about perfection."

Edison went to the keyboard, began an intro, and then launched into "If Ever I Would Leave You." He sang extra deeply, like Robert Goulet, whose baritone vocal range helped make the *Camelot* favorite a classic.

"Again, I know each detail of that particular summer as if it's a photo montage emblazoned in my brain," said Harry. "I can't say the same for even the beginning of this past summer. I know we all went to the beach. But did I wear my floppy hat or Mets hat or Key West hat or just the plain yellow one I ordered in the spring? On the other hand, I had on a colorful Roberto Clemente T-shirt that first day on census. I know this because it got me in the door of an apartment."

"You two get around," said Rosie. "Key West?"

"We never went there," said Carolyn. "He sometimes sends away and collects these things. Otherwise, gathers hats where we vacation. At least he does wear them."

"I also worry that other parts of me will be affected. What if I lose my memory and my body, too?" said Harry. "If it's something like MS, potentially I cannot use my hands or legs. Am I brave enough to write about this in a journal?"

"Like Bartlet on West Wing," said Edison, electing to pass on a response to Harry. "Except you're not president of the United States."

"Edison can't help himself," said Lola. "He's not trying to be mean-spirited, but his sense of humor is taking over."

"This Edison," said Edison, poking himself in the chest, "believes that self-awareness, which is so pivotal, needs a complement rather than a full-throated endorsement or denial. Music."

"It always comes back to that," said Rosie. "He genuinely feels that music is the best medicine for mind, body, and spirit. Isn't that right, Edison?"

Edison pretended to have a microphone and recited, "If music be the food of love, play on: Give me excess of it, that, surfeiting, the appetite may sicken, and so die." After the briefest pause, he said, "That was the famous one from *Twelfth Night*, but I prefer this one from *The Merchant of Venice*: 'The man hath no music in himself. Nor is not moved with concord of sweet sounds, is fit for treasons, stratagems, and spoils.' Every one of us has music in our souls. It's a matter of finding it, honing it, and nurturing it. I know it is the only means to return fully to health, Harry."

"Yes, I agree but I am an actual person, not a character in a play."

Lola took his hand, and Rosie, on cue, stepped around to massage Harry's shoulders and neck. Carolyn's lips parted, and she tried to smile as tears flooded her eyes.

"I wasn't aware of your Shakespearean self," Harry said to Edison. Harry had pigeonholed the man as being all about music all the time.

"Yes, later in life," was the reply. "I was in between long-term teaching gigs somewhere in the late 80s or early 90s. Since I learn not by reading but by listening, I found my way to the big library near Bryant Park and just sat with one LP after another of the plays. I was totally smitten, hypnotized, and went under with these for a long winter. As I dug deeper, I saw the way this man used music and how it was telling, revealing, in a variety of his plays."

"If I turn out to be a tragic hero, maybe go mad like Lear, you will bring me back with music, right, Edison?" Harry asked.

"Right, Kemosabe," Edison replied, doing his best to sound like Tonto. "We make-um peace together," he said.

Harry Reflects: 3

It's been just over a month since the family Labor Day party, and I've seen Edison three times—or is it four? Should I be worried that I cannot remember? Carolyn came twice.

I'm about as steady as a tiny paper sailboat caught in a gale. Drifting around is okay; the unknown is the true enemy. During my most uncertain times, restless in bed, I imagine the worst. Each bad dream ends with catastrophe: I am incapacitated; I am hospitalized; I am unable to proceed on my own. Should I hasten my demise?

Right now, I talk this out because I live in terror of the day when I cannot think, cannot express myself. Saying this again—this is my daily trauma. Why is this happening? What did I do? The other day, alone in the house, I took an old volleyball, mostly deflated, and threw it as hard as possible against the garage door, again and again. A dear and now deceased friend once told me that the best therapy during a frustrating time would be playing one-on-one basketball with a similarly sized friend:

person versus person. With the ball, it becomes me against whoever or whatever. Who or what crumbles first?

Edison is hellbent on music as the cure, and he wants Carolyn and me to actually make the music. We're not the same twenty-two-year-olds. Speaking for myself, I'm, at best, grizzled, fractured, and falling apart. Carolyn is putting up a good front, but I know this is wrecking her. She's jittery, nervous, but when you ask her, she says, "We signed up for everything together."

I keep going back to Stan Getz, my favorite sax player, and how he died. He and Kenny Barron toured together often, and both at the New Jersey club and in the city. I read something Barron wrote about Getz reacting to his cancer diagnosis by shifting to a macrobiotic diet and Chinese herbs. Stan actually was better for a while—maybe a year or more—and then he died. I don't know if I ought to go the Eastern medicine route. I mean, I'm not one to hope that arts and crafts will somehow help me retain physical touch and prolong my life in a cerebral middle lane; the situation wouldn't be fantastic, but it also wouldn't be fatal. I don't know why all of this Getz stuff is on my mind—maybe because of all the time I've spent in the jazz club. So many jazz musicians overdosed on drugs or became alcoholics. That came with the territory and maybe still does. It has to change. At the club, we didn't have to deal with it that much, maybe because the musicians knew they were in a suburb, where everyone pretends addiction is not a problem.

Okay, so Edison thinks music could be a preventive measure, if not a cure. What if, after forty-something years, I go back to my guitar or should I stay with drums? On occasion, I've amused the family with an occasional Beatles or Simon & Garfunkel rendition, but those times have been few and far between. I wonder what sort of teacher Edison would be. He's blunt and can be a pain in the ass, but he's also dedicated and, in his dry way, caring. I can be weary and start to feel small, as that song goes. I feel worst of all, at least when I am rational, for Carolyn. She's stayed with me, and now I may crumble into a vegetable of a human being. If she didn't take off when one of us could have, there's no way she'll bail now. God, I almost wish she would, to save herself, but that would mean I would become dependent on the girls. That I will not allow to happen. I would do pills before going down that road.

Getz was lucky he went so fast. Whatever I have doesn't sound like it takes me out in weeks or months. We could be talking years. Ugh. Go get your guitar, Harry, and wait for your fingers to stiffen so you can't pick or strum, can't do anything. No use talking chords because pretty soon you won't remember even a basic C chord.

Sisters

Marissa missed Grant and imagined marrying him. He was a solid person, loyal and not drippy. Diana, on the other hand, was relieved to be free of LG, whom she thought of as soggy as a wet log. That's what he was like: something that just sat there in the rain gathering moss without expending a smidgen of energy. A slug. Why, she mused, was she ever attracted to him? He was an okay lover but not all that sensational. He wasn't worth her effort; she was better off a few thousand miles away from him.

Neither of the sisters anticipated their newfound closeness. Not that they'd been distant, but their dad's potentially severe situation drew Marissa and Diana to each other. Growing up, Diana felt second in birth and second in talent. Sure, she ran track and emerged, during senior year of high school, as a tennis star. Marissa, though, was the performer both in school theater productions and as a solo vocalist. She was the lead sister in *Fiddler on the Roof* and played Juliet, too.

Marissa would have been satisfied to excel at just one sport. Her little sister had her pick. If Diana had so chosen, she could have been a softball player or, with her athleticism, a top volleyball player. Marissa had become more accepting of her womanly body. Still, it could present problems and her shape had long encouraged boys to flock her way. Warding them off became arduous and old. She wondered what it was like to be flatter and straighter.

The girls were no longer girls, and their roles were flipping. Here they were, back in the 'burbs looking after their parents, speculating about worst-case scenarios, and hoping for much better than that.

After the Labor Day festivities, Marissa spent much of her time at her place in Brooklyn and invited Diana to come and spend a night or two there as well. They tried to steer clear of stressful Harry-related conversation. Instead, they went out to listen to music or walked beneath the Brooklyn Bridge or enjoyed late dinners at Marissa's favorite go-to natural restaurant. Now, in contrast to their adolescent years, they were mutually pleased to be sister-friends. Spending a couple of days a week together was just the right amount of time. Diana had arrived at Marissa's on a blazingly sharp Sunday morning. Now, they readied themselves for the scene in New Jersey.

Harry and Carolyn, hoping to further cement the family unit, had been the ones to suggest this Columbus Day gathering. Again, Harry was looking for a theme. He convinced himself that this was both the intellectual and creative activity he needed to activate his brain and, more cogently, keep it functioning. He planned to ask Carolyn how she would feel about performing something with him. If she agreed, he would see if the daughters, too, might come up with something to share—on the spot, without advance notice.

"You want us to sing, Harry?" Carolyn had anticipated earlier in the morning.

"Good guess. You must know me."

"I choose," was her reply, and he nodded while smiling. "'Autumn in New York.' You think we can croon? Sinatra could, and that's the version I know. It's from some musical way back before we were born, I'm sure."

"I was just tossing the idea to you, like throwing a musical Frisbee. Never thought you would have a comeback answer right away. If I did, I would think Carole King or maybe a Motown. A schmaltzy ballad? Well, sure, we can try."

"It fits, Harry, and we're an hour from the city, after all. Here, I printed out the lyrics. Let me sing you the first stanza of the chorus." Harry nodded his approval as she did, so Carolyn continued. Soon enough, Harry joined in with some harmony—notes but not words.

"I love it," said Harry. "I wonder if we could memorize it," he added.

Carolyn waited a moment before responding.

"No need," she replied before it occurred to her that if Harry could memorize the words, it would feel like a huge win for him. She worried, though, that he might not succeed. Carolyn was relieved when Harry, instead, picked up the lyric page. "Autumn" pleased them both. Even if they'd not blended voices for some years, they knew each other's vocal range. To collaborate musically was to reminisce and enjoy.

"Why didn't we do this?" Harry asked.

"We did—maybe forty years ago, dear."

"James Taylor," said Harry. "That I remember perfectly."

Carolyn said, "'Fire and Rain' came out just before our summer, 1970, and we . . ."

". . . sang it together," he said, finishing Carolyn's thought. "At an open mic event Edison found for us." Harry started to laugh. "He actually brought microphones for all of us. Remember?"

Carolyn said, "Either he didn't trust the site or he's a perfectionist."

"Edison knows what he wants, however off the wall it is. He doesn't settle and I should follow that lead, try to be more like that. Gray areas can turn muddy for me just now."

"Or maybe not. Don't convince yourself of the worst, Harry. Why not look on the bright side?"

"These days it's avoidance of the dark for me. If that means emerging from a cave of emotions into rays of sunshine, however temporary, I'll take it. Fully light days are not on my horizon," he said, continuing with the imagery. "Carolyn, don't think that I don't want more—I do. It's just that everything is unknown. The more I read, the less I understand," he said, shaking his head.

She hugged him and held on.

"I'm just glad I'm with you, that we stayed together. Also, Edison and his insistence on music as, if not a cure, a helpful catalyst," said Harry.

"This is what I know, Harry," said Carolyn. "If you think you feel better, you probably are. Mind power cannot be understated. If you dread losing your memory, that path is set in motion and, well, it needs to be reversed. What say we try to impress the girls by singing 'Autumn' to them tonight? We have several hours to prepare. You haven't said a word to them about performing tonight. Are you sure you want to challenge them to sing as well? That is not exactly fair."

"Okay, so I toss this performance game at them but only with kindest intent," Harry replied. "It's probably best that I call them and ask if they might be able to perform something, yes?"

Carolyn nodded, hugged him again, and then kissed him. She remained silent but was gratified that they were giving their daughters advance notice. Carolyn overheard Harry on the phone detailing to Marissa the plot of the upcoming evening.

⁂

Diana and Marissa were taken by surprise but hardly stunned. Both started to laugh before Marissa said, "I guess he isn't too far gone if he's pulling this kind of thing."

"Yeah, same Dad. Harry with the hats, holiday themes, all of it. Probably a good thing. You know of any songs we can sing without practicing?" Diana asked.

"You know I've been in musicals, so I know lots of tunes. Lyrics, though? Forget it."

"Let's make up words to 'When You're Smiling,'" said Diana.

"What a fun idea, and maybe we can get Mom and Dad to join in and shift this to a group activity instead of a performance. What a great little sister you are," Marissa said before immediately launching into, "While you're sleeping, no more beeping and your mind will still be true."

Diana picked it up with, "Pleasant dreams with loving themes, they're surely sweetly true. And when I'm weary, dear, I look at you."

"We get tighter as days get brighter," said Marissa, "and laugh the full day through."

With that, the sisters embraced, having concocted a set of hybrid lyrics.

Diana drove the Subaru she had been leasing while she was in New Jersey, and they made their way to the old house that afternoon. On the drive, they tried to steer conversation toward the inconsequential since anything more might ultimately focus on their father.

This worked well until Marissa, who had been dozing, awakened and, without thinking, asked, "What about Mom if Dad goes away?"

"He will not just vanish, Issa," said Diana. "Whatever it is happens over years, sometimes many years."

"I read that, too, but what will she do? How will she handle that?"

"She was an amazing guidance counselor," said Diana. "She knows."

"They've been together forty years, and it's mostly been good," said Marissa. "She can't be the caretaker."

Diana started to cry and knew she could not continue driving. Her tears engulfing her, she managed to continue to a rest area. Her big sister hugged her hard, massaged her shoulders, and said, tellingly, "We'll take care of them; it's time." Then she sang,

"Take good care of my sis. Don't let her be blue."

Diana jumped right in with, "And when you do think of her, echo that we love her."

They joined together for "Wherever you are, whatever you do."

Diana dried her tears and said she could drive again.

They were braced for bumper-to-bumper traffic but were shocked to breeze into the suburbs of New Jersey without much trouble. Diana pulled into the driveway, and as they opened the doors, the sisters heard the parents harmonizing on "Blue Moon."

"For all we know, they've been at this for hours," said Marissa.

"Or else they just heard my car and decided to put on a show?" Diana wondered.

They found their parents sitting side by side on the piano bench at the old upright in the enclosed porch. Harry and Carolyn looked happy, cozy, glad to be squished against each other.

"How about some gallows humor for our event tonight, girls?" Harry said, glancing toward each of the three women in his life. "Maybe sing a song about the rewriting of our will."

"Harry, stop! The idea is to celebrate a holiday, even if it's a holiday that needs major revision," said Carolyn.

"My brain, what's evidently left of it, is trying to locate a new reality, first, and then cope," he answered. "Coping is what a will is about. I used to read Edgar Cayce, who was looking into life after the one on earth—you know, afterlife. That was all before this. Now, I go day one to day two and hope I get to double figures. All I can do is deal with what I have even though no one can say for sure what it is."

"Dad, Diana and I have been doing some research and it's not clear that you're losing your mind or marbles or anything like that. It's just that some things break down earlier in life than others," said Marissa.

"Part of me would rather if they said I had cancer. You have a choice to treat it or not. You know what it is. I don't even know who I am," said Harry.

Carolyn embraced him. "I do, and I love you," she said.

"'Love means never having to say you're sorry.' I can remember that and visualize Ryan O'Neal and Ali MacGraw in the movie. It's the more recent stuff that gives me trouble. That's why I obsess about Alzheimer's given what I read," said Harry. I'm not trying to be remorseful on a holiday gathering, but sometimes I'm so terrified that I feel like I'm in a vice grip."

"We're all here, Dad," said Diana. "Remember when I was little and you called me caterpillar?"

"Sometimes Special C. We had Special K cereal, so I did a takeoff on that," said Harry.

"Anyway, you would ask me what the worst thing that could happen would be. And I would always say . . ."

"Someone might step on me," said Harry. "Yes, I am not worried about getting trampled but about not being able to defend myself, protect you guys, and even be myself."

"Maybe we should get ready for later," said Carolyn in an effort to lighten the tenor of the conversation.

"When I told Edison all of this, he didn't blink an eye. He also immediately recommended music, and I do believe he thinks it can actually help. He's lived a life in limbo, what with each job leading either to the next or nowhere. To get by, he's needed to invent. Anyone know what I mean?"

"Just for this day, though, can we ease off?" Carolyn asked.

"I was impressed the one time I met him," said Marissa. "Dad, why don't you call him and see if he can come out here tonight?"

"I think he just likes being at his Houston Street place and occasionally going to the Village," said Harry.

"You always told us there's no harm in asking," said Diana.

When Harry called, Edison said he was interested. He was not, though, about to get into his garaged car, navigate his way to the suburbs, and then drive back late at night. It wouldn't work to get to a train. Thus, the idea was a no-go. Edison proposed that they assemble at his pad, as he called it, the following weekend. Harry quickly said yes before giving himself a chance to consider and possibly decline.

With Edison unable to make it, Harry, Carolyn, and the girls decided to enjoy the holiday as a family unit. All agreed to keep it easy, make it fun, not postulate about future unknowns. Harry and Carolyn realized that dwelling too much on hypotheticals was unwise, if not potentially destructive.

Harry said he would set up in the back-yard—chairs, an old boombox, the miniature electric keyboard utilized for these occasions. "I'll decorate, too, since everyone knows I like themes," he went on.

Carolyn was pleased to get some time without him and with her daughters. For the most part, she concealed her terror, but it was time to share, even if in an understated way, her concern about the future.

"I don't know whether I'm more frightened about his leaving us right away, like in a flash, or of a prolonged decline. Maybe that would be even worse if, by increments, he becomes a shell of who he was," she said. "Then I get embarrassed with my drama. I feel like I'm in the middle of a TV series or something—except that it's real."

"Mom, he's been your life for forty years," Marissa said.

"I just want to help," said Diana.

"Be yourselves with him. Don't be obsessed with how he is. He hates it when all the attention is on him. He wants to be a part of things, like always," said Carolyn. "He's out there getting it all ready for us. What I think is that he wants this new normal to be like the old normal."

The conversation continued until, out back, the sound of a crashing table startled the women. They went out back and found Harry sprawled upon the grass, the aluminum table toppled at an angle beside him.

Diana, the former high school runner, sprinted to him first. "You okay, Dad? What happened?"

"I don't really know," he said as the others arrived.

Carolyn cradled Harry's head. "So sorry, sweetie," she said. "You hurting?"

"Not a bit. Just puzzled," he said.

"Maybe we should go to the emergency room or one of those urgent care places just to get you checked out," said Marissa.

"I don't need that," Harry said, realizing that he was snapping. "I'm fine, okay?"

"Sure you are, but why did this happen and is it related to anything else going on?" Carolyn asked.

Harry waved her off and, dramatically dusting himself off as he regained his footing, resumed one of his favorite processes: preparing for a family party.

He came running back to the house with a wide smile on his face. The three women were trying for three-part harmony on "Mr. Sandman" when he tried to interrupt, but Marissa said, "Dad, just two lines." Carolyn, Marissa, and Diana sang the first portion together, and Harry laughed fully and without hesitation. They completed the verse with Mr. Sandman closing on the word dream.

Harry said, "Just about the coolest sound I've ever heard. Listen, the *Times* says there's a new drug for people with Alzheimer's. It's not a cure, but it dramatically slows down the process, the falling away," he explained and then began to sing, "Walk Away Renee."

All joined voices for the "follow back home" conclusion.

"I would sing this in Moab. No one knew it, and I couldn't believe it," said Diana. "The odd thing is this is one song LG knew. He had Beach Boys CDs like you, Dad."

"Maybe it's time to find another hat. By the way, it's not Beach Boys even if it sounds like that. It's a British group called Left Banke," said Harry as he turned to Diana. "Surfing songs in Moab?" Harry asked. "You never said your boyfriend was swivel-hipped or into cool music like Brian Wilson's."

"When we first met, he would bring out his stash of their tunes. Then we would be singing and swinging to them. It was really fun," said Diana.

"I'm thinking Edison," said Harry to Carolyn. "He could blast into the past with 'Surfer Girl.' But he's not here now, obviously. It's just us and no audience. Remember when you were little"—Harry looked from one of his daughters to the other—"and we used to make up lyrics? Your mom and I, urged on by Edison back in the dinosaur days, did that when the two of us were very young. That's why I pushed each one of you that way. Let's come up with some for 'Surfin' Safari'?"

No one responded, so Harry continued with "Let's all boogie now!" and Marissa burst out laughing.

"Talk like crazy, show us how."

To which Diana added, "Find a horse or ride a cow."

Carolyn finished the lyric with "Come, let's all visit Edison, gee."

Harry motioned to all and led with 'Safari' lyrics.

As everyone collapsed into chairs, he said, "They—I mean, the Beach Boys—would be proud of this idea, but those are the only words I remember. I used to know all the lyrics."

No one said a word. It was Harry who broke the uncomfortable silence by blurting out something having to do with holding hands, which was a cue for everyone to break into dance. Before they knew it, Harry had a Beach Boys CD poised for all-out catharsis: a happy and festive outcome on this Columbus Day.

When the night was still relatively young, Marissa and Diana retreated to respective childhood bedrooms, which retained years-old posters and stuffed animals. While the spaces now served other purposes, the girls' personal touches and even their individual auras distinctively marked each room.

Restless, Diana soon went to Marissa's room and sat on her big sister's bed which was wedged into a corner just as it had been when they were growing up. Diana picked up an old Cinderella doll, one of Marissa's treasured possessions.

"My foot would never fit the slipper," said Diana.

"Mine, either," said Marissa, "especially since I was cast as one of the wicked stepsisters in the musical."

"I don't remember you in 'Cinderella,'" said Diana.

"It was 'Into the Woods,' the spring production for my senior year in high school."

"Oh, yeah. That was when I knew you would be a movie star, Issa," Diana said. "You nailed that bitch and totally had the audience. And while we're on the subject of Prince Charming, what about Grant? Is he still back in Moab?"

"I'm thinking of asking him to move in with me in Brooklyn, but I'm not sure about the timing. This thing with Dad is dominating me, Dee."

"I wish I were in your position instead of figuring out how I can ditch LG for good even if I've already begun that process," she answered.

"Just because he's getting fat, Diana?"

"No, it's like that's a symbol that he doesn't care about his body and not really about me, either."

"Grant and I email or talk all the time. He is so far away, but I know his mind. What's best is his patience. I mean, he's been great ever since I told him I need some space because I'm so scared of this thing with Dad. I just don't know if I can balance it all, but I'm missing him and, well, you know."

"Wish I had that instead of a slug. I think it's pretty much over," said Diana.

Marissa hugged her sister. "I'm sorry, Dee," she said. "You don't want to waste all you are with him, though."

Diana, typically stoic, began to cry.

Part V

Chapter 9

Moab

Late Fall 2011

HARRY HOPED THE RED clay would rejuvenate him. He sent away for maps and brochures and went through them with diligence. It wasn't difficult to convince Carolyn to make a trip back to Moab. Through October, as the days grew shorter back home, he began to fret that this would either be his last fall or, worse, the last season he would remember.

Halloween had long before grown old and trying. Harry and Carolyn flew to the Southwest a day before, leaving the house to their daughters. They made it to Phoenix and, changing an old script, chose to fly to Denver, stay a night or two, and then drive five or six hours to Moab. They could go to Boulder, take it easy, and move on from there. This meant they'd have a slightly longer vacation.

In the books Harry had read, the Corona Arch Trail seemed perfect: medium difficulty, three hours for the whole experience, and abundant beauty. On the flight, he went on about details, and Carolyn was both impressed as well as wary. He was not quite the Harry she'd known since they were teenagers. On the surface, he seemed okay: Friends thought Harry looked fine and well, but Carolyn knew his recall was scant. Conceptualizing remained his strength until he needed a specific name or place and could not remember it.

Two days later, they were up early and determined to make it to Moab by evening. Harry had considered booking a room for a night at a place which had a pool and other amenities. That really did not make sense since they had the house — a second home forever.

Harry was aware that this might be the final occasion he was at the helm, commanding a trip. Over the years, they'd taken turns and, more recently, Carolyn had both initiated and planned. This time, however, he was determined to find another one of his selves. Harry and Carolyn had always talked of personal, political, and even emotional selves. Now, he urgently needed to find or salvage one lost intimate self. He fell asleep wondering how he would feel the next morning, whether his resolve would waver.

The next morning, they arose early and, after getting coffee and a few pastries, drove to the trail. Harry took Carolyn's hand as they began walking. He could not remember when he had last done so. Her fingers remained thin and tapered as opposed to his, which were now irregular, bumpy, but still serviceable. He would take it. If only his warped mind were still functional.

Pathways of sand occasionally interspersed with pavement, and one section included cables leading to a ladder. He prodded Carolyn, who took each step carefully and perched herself on the ground above. Harry grabbed a rung and placed both feet firmly on each foot strip as he ascended. Then, without warning, just as he was about to scale the final portion, metal came loose in his hand, and he grabbed for the side of the structure to avoid a ten-foot tumble. Carolyn immediately grabbed his hand and, with assistance, Harry made it to the top.

"That's how I feel about myself, Carolyn: Precariously, I get to the next day."

Instead of responding, she hugged him and pointed to her side. "You can see the configuration looks like a bow tie," she said, eagerly changing the subject.

"So it does. I remember the jazz group at the club, a trio, and for every performance each player wore a different bow tie. It was a preppie look, but they made it work," he said. "I'm okay. Let's keep going."

Carolyn took Harry's hand, and they made their way around some bends and along some stones. Just as Harry began to wonder how much farther they had to go, Corona Arch, spectacularly lit with sunshine, came into view. They kept going until reaching its base.

Harry said, "Let's lie down, just as they say."

With that, he and Carolyn briefly disengaged and, without anyone else around, went back-to-back on the red clay and sandstone. He took her hand, and she leaned over to kiss him. "This is why we came here, Harry," she said.

A sprinting black Lab broke the mood by licking each of their arms.

"Like the salt, buddy?" asked Harry.

Soon enough, two youthful adults with a tow-headed little girl running just ahead of them joined the black dog and the aging couple that was seated directly beneath Corona Arch.

"Sorry," said the father.

"No, he's just a delight, and we've had a few who looked like him and were probably part of his family," said Carolyn.

Nevertheless, it was time for the sixty-somethings to move on. After chatting briefly with the three humans and petting the pup, Harry and Carolyn ambled toward the trail that led back to the parking area.

"What are we doing?" Harry asked as he sat on a rock and beckoned Carolyn to do the same.

"Well, our hope is rejuvenation, isn't it dear," Carolyn stated rather than questioned. Harry did not respond, so Carolyn continued, "My hope was that this place, Moab, which is unlike anywhere we've been, could very well rekindle us."

Harry pointed to his head. "Whatever is loose up there just needs to be screwed in that much tighter. I think of Edison telling me to let the muse, the music, carry me. I try, but my brain isn't so much dysfunctional as it feels stuck. I hit a chord, and then I cannot move anywhere else."

"Okay, let's try this," Carolyn said and softly sang the first line of "The Sound of Silence." She urged Harry to join in, and he was pleased to remember the verses.

"I do flash back," said Harry, "when we did that as Edison played guitar in a tiny storefront in the Village, like, a hundred years ago."

"You're off only on the last part by about sixty years. This must have been 1971 or so," she replied. "You've still got it, Harry."

"Hello to some bit of darkness, indeed," he said.

"In contrast, the light out here on the red and brown rock just radiates warmth and even kindness to me," said Carolyn.

He nodded. "I agree. But Sweetness, if this is to be my final stretch of, well, being myself, I should be with our girls," said Harry. "I love it here, but another few days and we should return."

She put her arm around him, hugged him close, and said, "Homeward bound."

"Thank you, Paul Simon," he replied.

Chapter 10

Harry Reflects: 4

WHILE WORKING AT THE club, I used to hear jazz musicians talk about "the bridge." No one ever defined it, but everyone saw it as the catalyst, if not the capstone, of a piece. Did it link melody and solo, or did it bring the whole composition back to the original movement and tempo? Was it the stabilizer or the supplier of linkage? I never asked, never knew. I saw it as being similar to the roadway structure of the same name: It enabled me to get to the other side. Personally, I needed, desperately, to maintain stability, not lose it. I wondered where I could find a bridge to make that happen—a bridge to sustain sanity before I lost my mind. There. I had finally admitted it to myself. If I had Parkinson's, it would control me rather than the other way around. "No!" I yelled and then realized not a soul was within earshot.

No one will institutionalize me, no matter what. If this is the first sign of Parkinson's, I will not last the course. It's not like that time I ran a marathon when, past the point of exhaustion, I crumbled after I finished but then rose to embrace Carolyn and the kids, who were little then. Resilience was the name of that race, but this one ends, I read, with loss of bodily function. Not me, no. I will continue this conversation if only within my self-sealed vacuum.

Maybe they think I am a total blank page since I walk around seemingly baffled. I practice that face in front of the mirror till I have it down and can go to it whenever I please. It's no doubt a defense mechanism since this will be me and I will be it: perplexed at best and chaotically confused at worst.

Joni Mitchell was wrong—this life is not a circle game. Not mine, at least. I am always spiraling downward or upward when I would rather spin sideways. Wouldn't that be more Eastern—the idea of turning side to side and finally drifting away instead of landing with a deadly (forgive me) thud?

I know that I'm on the ground, on my side, and my head is heavy. Is that Shakespeare? Who is that caressing my hair?

❧ ☙

"Harry. Harry, dear," said Carolyn. "We need to go. We have to get back to the house."

"Edison," he said, "is my only hope for rejuvenation, even rebirth. I must see him again."

Carolyn surprised him with her reply: "It's so dramatic, Harry, when you say rebirth. I do hear you, though. Why only Edison? Unless I've lost my memory, that time capsule included Rosie and Lola as well. And you're leaving out your daughters?"

"No, you're right. I need Marissa and Diana there, too," he said.

"It sounds like you're already in the planning stage."

"We are three weeks till Thanksgiving. This would keep me busy: a project and finding a theme. You know," Harry said.

"Let's get back East, Harry. You're assuming people are available. Well, as far as I know, the grown-up girls are. Spending Thanksgiving at home is something we've kept up" said Carolyn.

They walked to the car, and Carolyn drove slowly.

"It might be the final time I see this wonder of the world," Harry said, simultaneously sighing and shaking his head sideways.

"My sweet man. You and I do not favor endings, I agree."

"Even when my mind was at its sharpest, I could never recall the ending of a book even a month after reading it. Something about The End gets to me. Maybe it symbolizes death."

While driving, Carolyn reached across for his hand and then, thinking better of it, pulled over to the side of the twisty road. She unbuckled her seat belt, leaned over, and kissed him softly on the lips.

"We've been together so long, but can this continue?" he asked.

Predictably, Marissa and Diana were the first to confirm that they would attend the Thanksgiving festivities, each fully expecting to spend the holiday in their childhood home.

Marissa had her place in Brooklyn while Diana stayed in her old room, relieved to be away from her boyfriend, whom she hoped to fully ditch. The older sister, though, wanted Grant to come to New York. Single life had its limitations, and harboring the dream of acting full time was wearying and stressful.

Harry was determined to get Edison to New Jersey, too. The man stayed close, these days, to his place on Houston Street. Harry needed a strategy or lure—Edison wouldn't make the twenty-mile journey for the hell of it. Since Harry knew Rosie would do her best to get everyone on board, he decided it made sense to first reach out to her. Harry wanted everyone around him, but he needed Edison. Rosie would be the linchpin holding the group together.

Thanksgiving—2011

"It's fucking cold in here," said Edison. "Can you please turn on the heat?"

Harry laughed more loudly than he had in weeks if not months.

Carolyn said, "Edison, watch your language. We're still young and impressionable."

Edison rolled his eyes. "Rosie was supposed to get Lola and then book it here. And yet I'm here, and they aren't. What gives? I hardly ever get in my car let alone drive to the fucking suburbs."

Marissa and Diana came in from the backyard.

"This is what I like: fifty-something degrees on Thanksgiving Day," said Marissa.

"When you live in Moab, you get that every year—even warmer," said Diana. "Hi, Edison. The outside slider was open, so we heard you. You're pretty cool. How old are you again?"

Edison spotted the old upright piano sitting in the dining room. "Methuselah was a thousand years old," he sang in his deep baritone voice. "That's all I can remember." Then a non-sequitur: "I knew something would be friendly here in the wilds," he said. Standing at the keyboard, he started to play "Happy Birthday." He stopped and said, "We can easily convert this to 'Happy Thanksgiving to Harry.'" Thus, Edison began again and everyone began to sing.

Early during the rendition, there was a knock on the front door. Before anyone could answer, Rosie and Lola, wearing matching deep-green sweaters embroidered with cornucopia goat horns filled with fruits and vegetables, walked in.

"We didn't want any turkeys bouncing around on our chests," said Rosie.

"We have enough sliding downward as it is," laughed Lola. "I'm not insulting our bodies; it's just the truth. You girls don't have such problems."

"It's best if we don't go there. Diana and I would kill for one another's bodies. Right, little sis?"

"Yeah. Having a goal of being skinny and never quite getting there hasn't been the most fun," said Diana. "You two, by the way," she added, looking at Rosie and Lola, "are incredible. Whatever your ages are, you look half."

"Everyone looks fine to me," said Harry. "If you don't mind, the menu includes hens, salmon, and some turkey, too. Not that we have an eighteen- or twenty-pound turkey, but there's plenty for any-one."

"And chocolate marshmallow cake, the Enten-mann's kind, for those who love sweets and already have tummies, like me," said Carolyn, patting her abdomen.

"Enough of this. It reminds me of my boyfriend, whose belly is so big he can't see over it to the floor," said Diana. "Let's do the day, okay, Daddy?"

"I almost devised an adult treasure hunt with what's left of my mind. You would have found that okay?" Harry asked.

"It would have been groovy," said Edison. "What did you decide on instead?"

While Rosie and Lola settled into the house by hugging everyone in sight, Harry disappeared. He returned several minutes later with a large blue-and-white–striped box.

"Just wanted to make sure I could find this where I stashed it a few days back. You know, Memory Boy here can forget," he said. "It is a game. That's my only hint. Girls, want to guess what's inside?"

"I just craved sports games, and Marissa was already into make-believe theater and then productions she put on for anyone in the neighborhood. I don't know. Monopoly?"

Harry laughed and shook his head as Marissa said, "Even when we were little, I wanted to do charades, but that isn't a board game."

Harry began to open the box, which contained a board game. He then extracted two smaller cardboard containers. "I had to go on eBay—you might know of it—and combine a few buys to compile all of this," he said. He then held up a cover.

Edison, Rosie, and Lola were silent. Carolyn, waving her arm like a conductor, led her daughters, who shouted, "Pirates and Travelers!" in unison.

Harry turned to his guests and said, "That's what we called it, but it's technically Pirate and Traveler. I had to go to extremes to find all of this stuff. It turns out Milton Bradley up in Springfield, Massachusetts, put our version out in 1936. There might have been even earlier ones, though. This was our family's favorite game. Right, girls? We learned geography through this old board," he continued. "See, if you go to Siberia, you find Yakutsk or Albany, Australia."

Edison suddenly came to life. "I bet you could find music from all over. Take Calcutta in India, and I bet it's on the map," he said. "Sitar and such. Mystical."

Diana squinted and said, "I never thought much about Greenland. Do people really live there, and how do you get there? You can't just take a plane, can you?"

"We could find out, maybe make some music," Edison continued. "The accordion is my new instrument. I just happen to have it in the back seat of my car."

"He's the same," Rosie said to Lola.

"Grayer but maybe younger," she replied.

Harry, laughing, said, "I brought all of you here to set fire to my brain."

"Honey, they haven't been around you all the time," Carolyn said. "You need to explain."

Diana, instead, jumped in. "My father wants a reboot, like for a computer," she said.

Harry added, "Actually, what I need is a new brain. But since I haven't heard of such a transplant, I have to deal with this malfunctioning model. Meanwhile, let's play Pirates and Travelers, our title for the game, with our rules."

"Yeah," said Marissa. "Groups or what?"

"I couple with my man," said Carolyn, who eyed Harry. "We're stuck together like glue."

"Sisters forever," said Diana.

"Lower East Side three, even if Lola defected," Edison (who had fetched the accordion, added.

Thus, the teams freelanced and found their way to gold in Dawson, Alaska; ostrich feathers near Cape Town, South Africa; silver in Denver, Colorado; and so forth. Everyone was more intrigued with the game board map, replete with golden, pink, yellow, and green coloring as numerous dots and linking lines connected the world's cities and countries.

"I only wish I were on that sailboat right in the middle of the Indian Ocean," said Edison.

"You?" asked Rosie. "It's tough to get you to go to another borough, and now you want to cross continents?"

"What I love about this game is that it's dated," said Harry. "Like me, but even older. Designed in 1936. Imagine that—even before Hitler and the war. Part of me imagines a time when we were not beholden to devices," he added. "The rest of me wonders how long I will be able to remember history, my life."

"As long as you can relate to jazz as you do, my friend, you're okay," said Edison.

"I don't know," Harry sighed. "Jazz, music I can do. I'm also pretty good about where Carolyn and I have been and the girls growing up, but each day is different." He shook his head.

"Dad," said Marissa, "do you really get stuck on things or is it more that you think you will?"

"I think it's mostly fear," said Diana. "I've been living here, and I see it. You probably can identify a lot of Miles Davis."

"I know the tracks from albums, concerts," said Harry.

Diana said, "It's not likely that you can nail what you jazz guys call a riff but can't get straight on, like, a take-out order"

"It's different, Di," said Carolyn, the only one in the family who called her by that nickname. Marissa often used Dee. "Dad is spot on when remembering the distant past, just not the more recent one."

"I'm sure I referred to it this way before, but it's like I have all my wires, only they get crossed," said Harry.

"You were a hyper boy even in 1970," said Lola.

"And sexy, too, with the curly, frizzy long hair and always sweating that summer," added Rosie. "I had the kids, and Richard worked the night shift. Thinking back, I'm surprised I didn't find some time to corner you."

Everyone, even Carolyn, laughed. She said, "I knew what a catch he was, still is. In some—almost all—ways, he's still sharp as a tack. Harry, free associate, okay? Moab."

"Arches," he said.

"Sexy."

"Carolyn," Harry replied.

"Music genius," Carolyn said.

Harry pointed at Edison, "Edison and then Monk."

Everyone laughed again.

"Census," Rosie said.

"Summer of 1970, Lower East Side, Houston." Harry looked at Carolyn before continuing, "I won't say it; she would be too embarrassed."

Lola said, "If you were just learning English and heard the word census, you might think it was kinky."

"Stop it," said Rosie. "I can understand why the younger generation"—she motioned toward Diana and Marissa—"finds this funny."

Edison cleared his throat. "Speaking of funny or hokey or cornball, what about a group sing of 'Country Roads' to lift the old roof off this house on Thanksgiving?"

"Actually, it's called 'Take Me Home, Country Roads,'" said Harry.

"My point is made," said Carolyn. "As the cliché goes, this one has a memory like an elephant."

"What?" asked Diana.

"It means I have exceptional recall," said Harry. "But that's only partially true."

With that, Edison lifted both arms, made eye contact with each individual in the room, and began to sing about heaven, West Virginia, the Blue Ridge Mountains, and the Shenandoah River. He paused, lowered his hands, lifted them again, and most everyone, knowing or partially faking, joined to sing about roads in the country leading back to West Virginia.

"Just a minute," said Marissa. "If we were singing about going to Moab, I would get it, but this group isn't exactly vintage hillbillies. We're saying that West Virginia is our place, our home? Not really."

"Your mother and I went there, to the Blue Ridge Mountains, and stayed in a cabin for a weekend after both of you girls were out of the house," said Harry.

"I wouldn't say the mountains were blue, but it was still very romantic," Carolyn added. "If Harry had his way, he'd probably squeeze those mountains into the Pirate and Traveler board."

"You know me too well," said Harry. "To change the subject, while I still have some of my marbles, I've been doing some reading about memory loss. It has something to do with blood flow, maybe to the brain? Anyway, it's called SPECT, which can send infrared light up here"—he pointed to his head—"so people like me can get more with the program."

"Like a broken record, I'll say again that music helps," said Edison.

"I'm not suggesting you're wrong, Ed. It's a combination of things. Plus, being around people I love doesn't hurt," said Harry.

With that, Edison started walking toward the front door. Over his shoulder, he said, "Just getting an acoustic I happened to bring."

"He really has much the same act," said Rosie.

"When I come to town, I can tell he's happy," Lola said. "Maybe his face shows his mood more than it used to."

"What do you say we make up the 'Scan and Brain' song?" Edison asked when he returned. When no one replied, he added, "This worked with high school kids. No pressure, just fun. And I will start with a riff off 'Oh, you can't get to heaven.'"

Marissa said, "We used to sing it both on car rides and at summer camp, so we know it really well."

"True," said Diana. "It's like Edison is zoned in on our family."

"Oh, you can get to heaven," Edison improvised, "on Harry's brain." At this point, he encouraged everyone to repeat that phrase before continuing, "Because Harry's brain"—they all joined in again—"is still quite sane. Oh, you can get to heaven on Harry's brain, cause Harry's brain is still quite sane, I ain't gonna grieve, my Lord, no more."

"I forgot about the religiosity," said Carolyn, "if that's a word."

"He plays, we sing," said Rosie.

"We try, those of us who are anywhere close to carrying a tune," added Lola.

"We sang a lot when we traveled in that old Vanagan," said Marissa. "Mom and Dad dragged us all over the place."

"I carried that forward to Moab," said Diana. "Hiking and singing, even with my ex-boyfriend."

"See," said Edison. "Music. And since no one else is offering, 'Oh you can't get to heaven on Eddy's stash." He rubbed his thin, white mustache. "Cause Eddy's stash smells just like hash." Edison urged everyone to join in, although the group response was a mixture of song spiced with laughter.

"Okay, so hash dominated the scene in the East Village way back when we were almost kids," said Harry. "As parents, though, you think your daughters might never have heard of it."

"Like it's part of corned beef hash, Dad? I've seen cans of that, sure, but come on," said Marissa. "On Thanksgiving?"

"Speaking of that, I'm in charge of the meal today," Carolyn said. "I wanted that part in this plan so Harry could take care of the day and its theme by himself without thinking of food. We would be close to eating turkey,, salmon, and the Cornish hens, too. Instead, though, let's delay."

"Then we won't be fighting the clock," said Edison.

"Time is what I'm up against," said Harry. "All of our brains clog with time. My struggle is to limit or outlive or even outwit, for that matter."

"There you are, my young friend," said Edison. "You're too smart for our cranial enemies."

"He is kind of young," said Carolyn.

"We always had a dad with a youthful outlook," Marissa added.

"I'd like to grow backward in that respect," Harry said. "You know, like take a magic pill to recover." He paused. "Even maintaining an even pace, like on a treadmill, would work. Sometimes, though, I feel like I'm falling off one."

"Man, I've felt like that forever," said Edison. "That is me, and maybe I was better off as a substitute. Doing the same thing every day? It sounds like a nightmare, man."

"More than that. When the circuits short out, I cannot fix them, cannot get them back to the 'on' position. You know what I mean?" Harry asked.

"I do much better with guitar strings. If I can place them where they should be, I just assume my fingers and brain will follow," said Edison.

"So that's why you curse the strings when you play sometimes," said Rosie.

Edison winked at her and, as he did so, saw Lola looking at him. She said, "Edison and his women. Always an attraction but never permanence."

"At least Harry and I were always in it for keeps," said Carolyn.

"This is when I remove myself to the backyard," said Marissa. "Dee, you going with me?"

"I'll let the next generation up talk about relationships. It's enough for me to figure out my own self these days," said Diana, getting up to join her sister.

As soon as they were outside, Marissa said, "I think he's terrified."

"About losing his mind? I know," replied Diana.

"What's going on with you, Diana?"

"Well, I'm single now, which is the way it was headed so no surprise there," Diana said.

"He wasn't the one for you. Grant's going to move in with me in Brooklyn. With all that's been going on here, we've been more physically apart. Now it's time to live in the same house."

"And I'm wondering if I can continue to stay here in my childhood room," said Diana. "I'm wondering about Mom and Dad, too. Sometimes, it's not clear which of them is going to crumble first, if you know what I mean."

"I've felt guilty for years, before you came back, living an hour away and not coming over here, like, every other night. I know that's ridiculous, but still. So where does that leave us? What we're both saying is that we need to move on. Do you want to go back to Moab? Is that your place now?"

"I like the way it looks and feels there. You know about my thing for being thin. I agree it's getting to be—no, it is—an obsession. Still, the rocks and the spare, almost bleak, look of the sky and stars—I long for that," said Diana.

"Do you think it would be okay if the two of us went there? I hate to say it, but the scene here is so stressful. Even if it was just for four or five days. We could do the sister bonding thing," Marissa answered.

"I think we need a plan," said Diana. "Like that old Pirate and Traveler board game Dad brought out. The places there, even from seventy or eighty years ago when someone came up with that game, are specific destinations."

"Arches is not?" asked Marissa.

"Okay, maybe not a plan but a map. Let's chart it out for Dad."

"For both of them. And I guess we really don't need a trip to Moab for that," Marissa added. "I was thinking that we could clear our heads out there."

"They're inside with those great old friends, and we should go back to everyone. You know how he likes the holidays," said Diana.

"Sure," said Marissa, and they joined arms to return. Marissa stopped her sister then and turned to her. "Now you got me thinking: It's a game that Dad needs. He's into gameplay and dredged up the Pirate one. What if we designed a new game?"

"Of both of their lives," said Diana. "Yes, but it cannot end since that's what he dreads."

"Ah, like theater games—and I've done some—about process and not victory. We should brainstorm, with laptops and legal pads, too," Marissa said as they walked back into the house.

"Youth," said Edison, "wherefore?"

"You're the one making up lyrics," said Marissa. "Anyone interested in a cycle-of-life board game?"

Edison looked upward and raised his arms as if searching for an answer.

He said, "No need for an elaborate invention since Harry brought out his game. Fellowship, yes; how so? By age or gender? Other suggestions welcome."

Carolyn said, "Edison, you're recommending we play and asking who we should divide into units instead of proceeding individually?"

Chapter 11

Harry: Finale

As he drove, Harry felt himself musing, thinking: Most of my marbles, as we used to call them, remain. I am not incapacitated, and my loved ones and family members are here. My wife, my daughters, Rosie and Lola from Houston Street. Edison and I, the two boys, are surrounded, outnumbered. But it's reality, not a game, and it's a struggle to stay sane. So stop with the remedies, the devices, the cures. No herbs, tea leaves, acupuncture, or even back massages.

When I was little and alone, I would play marbles by myself. We had a tin filled with them, and this was my primary collection. I finally found separate little plastic containers so I could group the marbles: bigger ones here; transparent beauties by themselves; solids like black, red, white, and purple in another holder; and so forth. I would try to make equal teams, and then I would be the shooter for both sides. There was never a winner or a loser, though, since as long as my fingers cooperated, it would all end fairly equally.

Maybe we should play marbles so I can test out my fingers. As far as I know, they are not my problem. That's probably the wrong word for it. "Condition" is more appropriate. I read where someone is donating $40 million to help solve what he called the Parkinson's condition. That's a better way to say it, but I'm not sure if anything takes away the feeling of dread.

I know what a metaphor is, but then I get confused. Let's say I take my ruby marble, one of those large ones, into the bathroom with me on any given day. I used to choose one and place it on the sink. Next, I would take a shower and come out to find it almost glowing through the steam I had just created. To calm my aching back, one doc advised jacking up the heat to assist with flexibility. This means departing the shower and walking into a cloud of mist. But my marble, when I do this, always shines through the fog.

The other morning, though, I came out of the shower, looked at the forest green marble which I somehow had in the bathroom, and, well, was confused. So I put my clothes on and went out to eat breakfast. An hour later, it came to me that I'd forgotten to shave. This is a time when stubble is fashionable, and I'm still not comfortable with that.

The inner controller, the hidden wizard, loses his power. After that Houston Street period when I was adrift, I took an acting class. It was then that I learned to disguise and camouflage my feelings. I created different masks to conceal anxiety and pain. Until recently, that trickery succeeded.

Let me take you inside of me, as my brain struggles to survive. You know the scrim used for live stage productions everywhere? During my brief high school theater period, I was once drafted into a tech group responsible for getting this skinny, gauzy screen set up. I found out that one kind was actually called Chameleon. Can you imagine? I always wanted to be a person who could adapt and make the best of a difficult circumstance. When I was young, I had these different expressions and looks, like with the long hair during the Lower East Side summertime way back. I wanted to have these facial options, but I wanted, also, for people to know who I was. That's a lot to ask of a brain.

Mine did it for such a long time, bearing with me as I moved from one person, on the outside, to the next. These days, when I think of my brain, I imagine puzzle pieces that fit exactly but are fast coming unglued. Does anyone have a clamp to be certain they stay in place?

I had a dream that I was in a deep cave and my brain was at the top in sunlight. But I was stuck, wearing smooth-soled shoes, unable to scale any walls. And it was like a well; there were no steps. There was a percussive sound like people on the outside were banging rhythms: dum, dum, dum. Then the sound was repeated. I was desperate to wake up.

I know: We all fall down, tumble into holes, get depressed. My brain or a combination of brain and will could always coalesce to lift me away from the abyss—until the past year or so. You know how when you lift something heavy, like a couch, you bend your knees so you don't pull anything? Well, I often practiced that with my mind. I felt like I could approach it by increments to make it work, to be accurate.

Can it be that I've forgotten how to do that and another force is dominating and dictating? I no longer have any say. Worse, I feel like a victim of my own ineptitude. At this moment, I disappoint every human being I care about. I'm quite aware of what goes on during a conversation. People cannot see whatever it is inside of me that is seriously out of kilter, off the grid. That something is me.

While I am able, I'm recording this for those closest to me, the dear souls who were at yesterday's gathering. Edison, you've said before that music might be a key—but to what? Recovery, knowledge, answers, perspective, calm? I will take any of the above or in combination. Do you still have the bong from forty years ago? What was in that thing? I know you cannot answer, but I do wish to hear about the therapeutic music part at length because this journey is about to become more solitary.

Who knows what degenerative effects the mind suffers? I realize this sounds hifalutin, and I don't mean to come off like a pompous ass. As of this moment, I still can reason so I might as well ask questions and, forgive me, make pronouncements. I still know what a non sequitur is, so here goes. But maybe it isn't since I started my statement talking about this. Who spun this web, this thing that cannot be disassembled? Further, have I contributed a strand or two? You notice that I keep posing questions even as I am certain no one has satisfactory answers. My brain feels caged in, like when you're landlocked. Maybe that's it: I need, for God's sake, to free it, to liberate myself.

Like that time we took a vacation to southern Maine and went to a beach unlike those I knew. It had no sand; how can you call it a beach? It had the name Gooseneck and was definitely strewn with rocks, one of which tripped me and practically cut off one of my toes. Who cares, at this point, about toes? Then, though, I wanted to go for a swim. So, we drove south on US 1 through towns like Kennebunk and Wells before reaching a really touristy place that I wanted, for the longest time afterward, to call Podunk. It's not a word like that but it had "hunk" or "qunk" or something like that at the end of it. This is where my mind breaks down and, regardless of what they tell me, you cannot soft-pedal; the spiral goes straight down. Better that I think of that charming Maine town where the sandy beach stretches forever. Ogunquit! Suddenly, this comes to me, along with a visual, as we used to say about early television pictures, in color.

I was up at five in the morning and didn't want to wake Carolyn, so I went for a walk on the beach. It was nearly empty, just a lonely fisherman. I went to the right of him; I remember that, don't ask me why. I was by myself, and the sun wasn't up yet. Suddenly, something flew out of the water, like at an angle, and I jogged to see it better. The creature did it again. It was huge! I told Carolyn about it later, and we agreed that whatever I saw flying was new for us. At 10:00, I went to the visitors' booth for the town and they said it was probably a humpback whale and that whales were friendly and to rejoice. They showed me a photograph and, yes, there it was: the breathtaking stunner of a whale, just like the one I saw.

Lately, I've done some research about humpbacks because that image keeps coming back to me in my sleep. What I discovered is that their brains are much bigger than ours. This came as a shock, but the rest I could have imagined—that they were in touch through their tails and through that breaching thing where they just leap out of the water. I can imagine Edison writing a song about that. I can even see him strumming and singing as those glorious dancers come leaping out of the waves. They sing, too, so maybe if Ed came up with something, they would join in. That would be something. I bet one humpback is actually talking to another when we think it's just a random sound to enjoy. Maybe they're swimming in the waters like on the Pirate and Traveler board. I know, not really, but this is still what I do—imagine.

Like Mr. I. Magination from when I was a kid. Remember? I was just old enough to watch the end of this sometime in the early 1950s. He was the man with the magic reputation—at least, that's what he claimed. I'm sure I didn't know what reputation even meant. He had this little train and took kids to an imaginary town. It's so clear to me. Actual people were singing live; it wasn't animation. I loved that. I'm not sure what all of this means and why I'm seeing this right now when I don't even trust myself to drive. It's not the driving, but where am I supposed to be going? The connection is that they have a board on the TV with the names of countries and, I think, of Pirate and Traveler.

I dream about the best things in my life: Carolyn; the girls; Edison, Rosie, and Lola. Not about death and dying. Those blasts do haunt me when I'm awake. When they do, I fight them off and try to go back to sleep by allowing Mr. I. Magination to conjure Moab and Arches and all of that beauty. Can he really be doing something for a person whose mind is fractured? On the other hand, I would love to hear Edison spin something off I. Magination's original tune. Many people think Ed's quirky, but that's why he can write lyrics. He doesn't think in a straight line; he's not boring.

Neither am I, but I'm not totally there and not going to be totally anywhere. I heard Carolyn the other day giving report card marks about me. "No, it's not his movement and he's fine in a conversation. He just gets fuzzy with details, recent ones especially." That I can repeat with precision.

But with the rest, it's kind to say fuzzy. When you crack a bone, you probably get a cast. When your mind breaks, they say it isn't so bad, but it is. Don't try it.

Awakening

Suddenly, he roused himself, aware that he'd dozed off among friends.

"We do need Pirate and Traveler but not Moab. Not exactly. Let me get the game," he said and disappeared for a couple of minutes before returning with it under his arm. "On second thought, I want to be a kid again, and you're my family and closest friends. Let's go to this playground that's nearby. It's not really done yet, but it's good enough so we can play."

"You sound like the young guy who visited us forty years ago and came to stay on Houston Street," said Lola.

"I will bring my guitar," Edison added as Carolyn smiled broadly.

"If there are swings, I'll be happy," said Diana.

"And I haven't gone down a slide since when?" Marissa asked.

"Since you were around fifteen," said Carolyn. "We just discovered this place the other day. Some, but not all, of the equipment is up, and some is just kind of waiting around."

"A caravan!" shouted Harry, leading people out of the house and to the cars. "Follow me, and if you get lost, well, I don't know what to tell you since I'm lost. To the blue playground!" he implored and opened the passenger door for Carolyn.

Diana said, "We're right behind you," as they slid into Marissa's old VW Cabrio. Marissa quickly flipped the top to convertible status.

"As usual, the three of us are together," said Lola, ushering in Edison and Rosie. "Amigos forever, and let's see if I can keep up. Otherwise, we'll never get to this place."

Harry drove quickly, taking shortcuts through neighborhoods before coming to a cul-de-sac where houses were in the process of being constructed. Since it was late in the afternoon on Thanksgiving, no one was out and about. The cars parked in a semicircle. Harry motioned for all to follow him, and he brought them to a small path at the beginning of the brush and long weeds.

"I knew I shouldn't have gone to the country on such a holiday," said Edison.

Harry took off sprinting as Carolyn made circular motions around her head in an assessment of his antics. She called behind to her daughters, "Look! This is the first time he's been his old self in how long?"

Marissa grinned while Diana said, "Hey I was the track star. Should I try to beat him like when I was in high school and we used to race?" She loped gently ahead and caught up to her father because he had slowed at an opening and was gazing into the distance.

"What, Dad?" asked Diana. Then she saw the mixed floral of green and purple, framed by trees.

"This could be New Jersey's answer to *Field of Dreams*," he said. "We don't need Costner or James Earl Jones." He took his younger daughter's hand, and they walked on.

"Look," said Harry. "Some kids put a version of home plate here."

As they knelt to examine the placement, banjo music played. "I decided to bring this along instead of my guitar," said Edison. "I was planning on something like 'Turkey in the Straw,' but I can finagle chords for that baseball game song we all know and love." The friends came together for a chorus unto themselves. Everyone else in the neighborhood on this mild Thanksgiving Day seemed to be inside preparing to eat and drink.

"In just a moment, we'll put down the rest of the bases," said Harry.

"He hasn't been like this in, what, a year? Two?" Carolyn said while laughing.

Edison strummed all into "Take Me Out to the Ball Game" as Marissa and Diana joined arms. Lola followed Rosie on a right-angle course from home plate.

"That's it," said Harry. "Here's a sponge for first base."

"Ridiculous," said Rosie. "What if it rains?"

"Then we go to 'Singin' in the Rain,'" said Lola. "Right, Edison?"

"Ah, a classic, and I used to practice the Gene Kelly part," he added. "Watch." He leapt off the ground perhaps an inch or two and clicked his heels together.

"That looks like Judy Garland in *The Wizard of Oz*," said Rosie.

"I'll take it," said Harry and implored everyone to follow him around the bases.

It had rained earlier that week before a short cold spell hit, and now it was nearly sixty degrees.

The ensemble took its time circling the field while somehow traversing the ruts, bumps, and further obstacles the ground presented. Edison, with his banjo, ambled behind as he launched into The Beatles's "In My Life." He caught up to the others, who were happy to pause and join in song.

"Yes, there are many places I still do remember," said Harry, "and this one is a new favorite. I wouldn't mind spending much of my life in a field like this. I don't want to end up in some institution wasting away. Let's play some baseball. It's a lot better than arts and crafts. Follow me." He led them to a plastic storage crate and opened it. Inside were three canvas bases and what appeared to be a regulation-size home plate. "Come on!" Harry chortled, and Carolyn ushered the group. "Here, take these," he said, distributing the bases and holding up baseball gloves, bats, and a ball. "The concession I make is using a softball and not a rock-solid hardball."

Edison draped his banjo across his body and grabbed the plate while Rosie and Lola placed the bases in approximate areas of first, second, and third. Harry, gleaming, put on a red ball cap without a logo, drew it over his eyes, and sang, "It's a lovely day for a ball game, and then we begin the smorgasbord back at home. Best Thanksgiving ever!" Smiling from ear to ear, he continued, "Some life, wouldn't you say?"

Acknowledgements

Mike Moran continues, as a primary early reader, to support my work, understand its place and purpose, and keenly respond to characters. He is an invaluable asset whom I trust.

Erin Binney edits my fiction with both a discerning eye and care for the people inhabiting the novels. As such, she is an indispensable member of this team.

Amy Brantley, proofreader, locates what I've missed. Further, she assists with content.

Dar Albert provides the catchy and appropriate cover art.

Christine Richardson pulls together all of the elements and in so doing expertly formats the final product.

My family continues to stand behind and for me as I explore a later-in-life career as a novelist. Thanks, first, to Betsy, with whom I've shared more than a half century. Our sons, Jason and Scott, are always there for us as are daughters-in-law, Nina and Ashley. The remarkable grandchildren (Allison, Summer, and Arlo) have a recent addition, Violet Lillian Sokol, around eight or nine months of age as this book appears. Violet reinvigorates all of us. May she, her brother, Arlo, and their cousins Allison and Summer enjoy happy, lengthy, meaningful lives.

I surely appreciate readers' positive responses to previous novels. More thanks to my close friends who are virtually in my corner as I move forward with several other projects.

About the Author

FRED SOKOL, IN SEMI-RE-TIREMENT, writes novels and plays as he continues to review professional theater for His previous books include "Mendel and Morris," "Destiny," and "Silverbirch Summer." He also co-authored "Muses in Arcadia: Cultural Life in the Berkshires." Fred has scripted "The Forever Boys," "The Lewis Sisters" and has another play in the works. As an arts journalist, he has reviewed a few thousand plays and has interviewed such artists as Idina Menzel, Christopher Reeve, William Styron, Joanne Woodward, Bernadette Peters, Mandy Patinkin, Arlo Guthrie, Dizzy Gillespie, Olympia Dukakis, Vanessa Redgrave, August Wilson, Ethan Hawke, Suzanne Vega, Savion Glover, Martha Reeves and Susan Sarandon. He also interviewed Bob Cousy, Julius Erving, Scott Hamilton — and Bill Moyers. He was founding editor of The Connecticut Quarterly.

As a theater leader at Asnuntuck Community College, American International College and Bay Path University, Fred directed 45 productions. He intends, one way or another, to stage another show.

Fred and his wife, Betsy, live in Longmeadow, Massachusetts.